There's a
Spaceship
in My Tree!

ZONDERKIDZ

There's a Spaceship in My Tree!
Copyright © 2008 by Robert West
Illustrations © 2008 by C.B. Canga

Requests for information should be addressed to:

Zonderkidz, 3900 Sparks Drive SE, Grand Rapids, Michigan 49546

Library of Congress Cataloging-in-Publication Data

West, Robert. –
        There's a spaceship in my tree!/ by Robert West.
            p. cm. – (Star-fighters of Murphy Street ; bk. 1)
        Includes bibliographical references.
        ISBN 978-0-310-71425-5 (softcover)
        [1. Science fiction. 2. Christian life – Fiction.] I. Title. II. Title: There is a spaceship in my tree.
PZ7.W51933Th 2008
[Fic] – dc22

                                                                    2008007360

Published in association with the literary agency of WordServe Literary Group, Ltd., 10152 S. Knoll Circle, Highlands Ranch, CO 80130.

Zonderkidz is a trademark of Zondervan.

Editor: Barbara Scott
Art direction & cover design: Merit Kathan
Interior design: Carlos Eluterio Estrada

The Star-Fighters of Murphy Street

There's a Spaceship in My Tree!

Robert West

ZONDER**kidz**

For my dad, Earl West, whose life of integrity, faith, scholarship, and quiet strength is a challenging example to follow.

-RW

Table of Contents

1

Alien

Beamer was an alien. He wasn't a ten-legged slime bag with fourteen eyes, unless, of course, you believed his big sister. Still, Beamer was an alien—no question about it. He didn't belong here. He couldn't even breathe here.

His mom said it was just the humidity. Sure! Methane was more like it! When they found his shriveled, oxygen-deprived body, they'd be sorry.

Now he'd been sent to some place called a cellar—clearly an alien environment. Nobody in California had a cellar.

Beyond the small pool of murky light at the foot of the steps, a heavy gloom spread out across the room like a fog bank. He stepped down from the last creaking step. "Hey!" he yelped, recoiling back up the step. "What *is* this stuff?"

He kneeled down to test the floor with his fingers. *Weird, man ... spongy, like maybe it wasn't a floor at all but something alive, like a tongue for something with a digestive system!*

Dust was what it really was—several years' buildup. Beamer stepped down again hesitantly, sending a puff of it into the air. The wind outside picked up, rattling the high, grime-coated windows. The structure above him creaked and groaned like a cranky old woman.

Then something scritched and scratched. He turned ... and froze!

It was huge, with tentacles attached to a disgustingly bloated body. Not a second too soon, Beamer dived to the floor to avoid a twisted tentacle reaching over his head.

Now, point-blank in front of him, was a large bin of shiny, black rocks—no doubt the shrunken, dehydrated remains of creatures the beast had already devoured.

Beamer scooted back frantically on all fours. At the same moment, a high whining sound came from behind. He lurched to his feet and whirled around, bumping into a cart, which sped rapidly away. Suddenly he was pelted in the face by a strangely filmy object. A moment later he was wrestling with an entire barrage of filmy, flimsy, smelly things.

Aiiii! Germ warfare! his mind screamed.

There was a screech. "*Yiiiii!*" Beamer yelped, as a small creature flashed by. It leapt to a table and fled through a break in a window.

Beamer shot up the steps like a missile and blew through a door into a short hallway. He slammed the door behind him and leaned against the opposite wall, breathing heavily.

"Mother!" A shrill voice from upstairs brought him spinning around in panic. "Did you know they've got a vacuum laundry chute up here?" The voice continued. "Shoots clothes down to the basement like spit wads!"

Alien

Beamer's mother stood in the entryway wearing tattered, cut-off overalls and a tool belt. "Well, at least something works around here. Beamer!" she exclaimed in amazement, "What are you wearing on your ear?"

"Huh?" Beamer removed a pair of girl's underwear from his left ear— *Vacuum laundry chute? Whoever heard of a vacuum laundry chute?*—and threw them down disgustedly.

"Hey, Mom!" the shrill voice called again. "I can't find my pink Nikes." It was Beamer's big sister, Erin. At fourteen going on fifteen, she was God's self-proclaimed gift to the ninth grade. Of course, that was back in Katunga Beach. Middleton was a whole new ball game.

That's what this alien world was called—Middleton—a middle-sized city in a middle-sized state, smack dab in the middle of Middle America—a thousand miles from the nearest beach!

Only a week ago, Beamer was hanging out in a cool, high-rolling suburb of L.A. on the cutting edge of the early teen set. Now he was carting boxes around a broken-down house in a prehistoric neighborhood on an ancient street probably named for somebody's dog. Murphy Street. It certainly wasn't Shadow Beach Lane.

Beamer scrunched up his nose. The house even smelled old—as in fossilized. The discovery of an electrical outlet had been a great relief. He wasn't sure Xbox came in a windup version.

He banged through the screen door onto the front porch and picked up another carton. His mother was standing there, holding a scraggly plant in a pig-shaped pot.

The lady realtor who had given it to her was bustling toward her car, her mouth on auto-speak. "If you run into anything unusual," she called, "don't panic. I'm sure it's not dangerous. The previous residents were ... uh ... different—scientists or rock singers or something—but harmless. Anyway, just call if you have a question."

"I will," Beamer's mother responded absently, still looking in bewilderment at the ugly pot.

Beamer looked at the ramshackle porch swing and the peeling paint around the windows. *Rock singers in this dive? Who did she think she was kidding?* Then again, that same lady had managed to sell this overgrown pile of bricks to his otherwise genetically superior parents.

Beamer MacIntyre shifted the box in his arms, pried open the screen door with his pinkie, and spun through into the house. The antique door immediately fell off its hinges. Mrs. MacIntyre, or Dr. Mac, as her kiddie patients called her, groaned and pulled a screwdriver from her tool belt.

Beamer trudged slowly up the staircase with his load. "Move, you dunderhead," his sister growled as she pounded down past him like an avalanche. "Mother, isn't this place air-conditioned? I'm about to die!"

"It's the humidity, honey," her mother answered. "You'll get used to it."

"Mo-o-o-o-ommm!" Erin wailed, charging into the crate-littered living room. "D'you mean there's no air-conditioning?!"

"No, I mean you'll get used to the humidity," Dr. Mac replied. "Air-conditioning is being installed—one for upstairs and one for downstairs. Your father is out arranging things now. Last I heard the downstairs one will be working tomorrow."

"What about the upstairs one?" Erin asked with a shrill note of panic.

"Uhm ... not for a couple of weeks, I'm afraid."

"Weeks!!! So I'm supposed to wake up every morning with

Alien

my hair dripping? That does it; I can't start school—not 'til the air conditioner's working."

"Calm down, honey," her mother said. "Your hair always looks just fine. I'm more concerned about whether that oversized octopus of a coal-burning, water-heating furnace in the basement will keep us warm in winter."

Octopus? Furnace?! Beamer cast a glance down at the basement door, his cheeks picking up a definite reddish glow. *Oh great! So I had a battle with a furnace! What were those little black things then? At least nobody saw me ... I hope.*

"Now go finish unpacking. I'm sure your shoes will show up," Dr. Mac said, turning her daughter around and pointing her back up the steps. "Go on."

Erin groaned and lumbered up the staircase, then accelerated past Beamer to the top. She triumphantly stuck her tongue out at him and yanked open a door.

Beamer finally reached the second floor. Straight ahead was a wide but short hallway with two doors on the left and one on the right that opened into bedrooms. Immediately to the right of the staircase was a short, narrow hallway that led to the upstairs bathroom and a spare bedroom beyond. He kicked open the door to his room—the second one on the left—and promptly tripped over something in the doorway. "Oomph!" he gasped as he and the box's contents simultaneously thudded to the floor.

Groaning, he propped himself up to see the spilled items strewn, like a comet's tail, across the floor toward the tall, twin front windows. Through a window he noticed clouds gathering above the rooftops. *Back in L.A. we had rain programmed down to just one season a year. Here I am, two time zones and half a continent away from home.* "Marooned in Middle America," he moaned out loud. "I'd rather be on Mars."

Suddenly a blood-curdling scream shook the windows. It sounded like his big sister was in trouble, which meant it also sounded like fun. He charged into the hallway and saw a door that he hadn't noticed before that was nestled in that narrow hall next to the main staircase. The door was now open, revealing a narrow set of steps going up. He careened up the stairs and saw Erin standing off to the side, frozen in place, eyes glazed over like she'd been zapped with a stun gun.

"Hey, Erin, what's the matter?" he taunted her. "See an itsy-bitsy—" Then he saw it. "Awesome!" he gasped.

Their nine-year-old brother, Michael, clattered up the stairs on his hands and feet like a cocker spaniel, followed by their mom, who was tightly gripping a vicious-looking broom. They too caught Erin's freeze-dried expression and tracked along her sight line.

2

Mutants in the Attic

It was a spiderweb roughly the size of Texas.
One thing was for sure, whatever bloodsucker spun
that thing must have had a toxic waste dump for an
incubator. Soaring from floor to the apex of the roof, it
spread across the attic like a see-through wall.

"Mo-o-o-o-ommm," whimpered Erin, her voice
trembling. "I . . . can't . . . moooove."

"Don't worry, honey, I'm right here," her mother
said, unconsciously backing toward the stairway. "Just
step back slowly."

Erin hesitantly slid one foot back.

"I'll get my Power Blaster 150," Michael
announced, and scampered down the stairs.

"I saw this strange shadow across the ceiling, so I
came up to see what it was. Then I turned around,"
Erin said, pointing at the web.

"Lady! Where do you want the piano?" a gravelly
voice interrupted from downstairs.

With a wary glance at the spider metropolis, Dr. Mac hurried down the steps. "Come on, kids, we've got a lot to do before Dad gets home."

"But what about the web?" Beamer asked.

Their mother stopped halfway down. "Uh ... tear it down, I suppose."

As their mother disappeared below, Erin gave Beamer a *no-way!* glance, silently mouthing the words, "Tear it down?"

"Yeah ... right." Beamer said, looking anxiously at the web looming above them. "That dude falls on you, and you'll spend forty years getting unwrapped."

At that moment, a sunbeam broke free of a cloud and flooded the tall windows like a waterfall, lighting up that wispy silk curtain like a giant sunburst.

"Hey, look!" he exclaimed, suddenly noticing two long, dust-covered tables on the far side of the web. Scattered across them were broken and discarded test tubes and chemical beakers and a stack of electric cables. Remembering what the realtor had said about scientists, Beamer said in a hushed voice, "What if it's a mutant spider created by some evil genius who used to live here?"

"Aw, get off it," Erin drawled nervously, already backpedaling toward the stairs, her eyes fearfully searching the dark corners of the attic. "I've got an idea. Let's leave it to Dad."

"Sounds good to me," Beamer said, relieved. "Let's get out of here."

The web quivered and the test tubes rattled as the kids plummeted down the steps.

* * * * *

By dinnertime the Tale of the Web had grown into an epic story of courage and adventure. According to Beamer, he had narrowly saved his sister from having her life juices sucked out. Erin, of course, hotly disputed this account.

For his part, their dad, otherwise known as Mr. Mac, looked a little green when he came down from his first look at the web. Several phone calls later, he had arranged for a bug scientist—an entomologist, that is—from the university to come out and have a look. In the meantime, the attic was quarantined—off-limits.

The MacIntyres celebrated their first day in the new house with a candlelight dinner. Actually, *celebrate* was too strong a word. For one thing, they ate at tables that were packing boxes—a different size for each person in the family, like *Goldilocks and the Three Bears*.

For another thing—and the real reason for the candlelight—there were no light switches. In fact, none of the electrical appliances worked, which wasn't surprising since they had no on/off switches. At first they thought it was the electricity, but then Dr. Mac plugged her drill into an outlet and it worked just fine

"They can't do anything right in this town!" Beamer complained. "Nothing works, the air's thick enough to choke on, and everything's old and falling apart."

"I bet there's not a decent mall within twenty miles," Erin chimed in.

"There's a great park a block over!" Michael said. This note of cheer stopped everyone cold. Beamer and Erin looked at him like he had just dropped off the Big Dipper.

"Well, it's true. One block that-a-way," he pointed. "It's even got a zoo!"

"Right, squid head," Beamer snapped at him. "And

Disneyland is in the backyard."

"Nobody ever listens to me," Michael muttered to himself as he reached for an abandoned taco on Erin's plate.

"I wish we hadn't come here!" Beamer said, banging his hand on the box.

"Me too," Erin joined in. "How am I going to make cheerleader here in front of dorks who don't even talk right. It's y'all this and y'all that," she said, mimicking the local speech, "and wee-uull sumbody pulease tunn the laats ahwn!"

Blink! The chandelier suddenly lit up like Christmas!

"Who did that?" Erin exclaimed as she whirled around.

3

Things that Go Blink in the Night

Mr. Mac disappeared through the kitchen door and reappeared, moments later, through the hallway portal. He eyed the chandelier thoughtfully. "Hmmm ... Erin, would you say that again, only with the word *off* instead of *on*?"

"Uh ... what? D'you mean ... uh, lights off!" she said with a puzzled look. Nothing happened.

"Ho! This is very interesting." he mused. "Erin, try it again, saying it the same way you did the first time—with the accent."

"Oh ... well ... sure," she stammered, searching for the words. "Let's see ... uh ... laats ... uh ... awf. Laats awf!" she said louder.

Immediately the lights went off.

"Hey!" Erin giggled. "Laats ahwn!" They came on again.

"The realtor said the previous owners were ... unusual," Dr. Mac commented as she stood up, "but a house you talk to?"

"And with an accent, at that," Mr. Mac laughed.

"Laats awf!" Michael yelled. Dutifully the chandelier went dark.

"Laats ahwn!" Beamer joined the game. They came back on.

"Laats aw—" Erin started.

"Hey! Hey!" their dad interrupted. "Let's hold up on the light show before we either talk the thing to death or go blind."

"See," Beamer's mom said, tossing her usual sunny-side-up attitude into the dispute, "everything's not so bad."

No one can ever have a decent fight in this household, thought Beamer.

"There'll be lots of new, fun things happening here," his mom continued.

"A one-trick light switch does not a happy home make," Erin grumbled.

"No, that's true," their dad agreed. "There's a lot more to making a home than living in a house."

"Unless the Lord builds the house, its builders labor in vain," their mom said. "That's from someplace in the Psalms, I think. God's given us a good start. Your dad has a good job at the university. Things are getting off the ground for my pediatrics clinic. We'll be starting out at a new church Sunday, and school's only a couple of weeks off."

"School?" the kids groaned in unison.

Mr. Mac picked up his napkin and wiped his chin. "I know it's tough, guys, making this move. But you've got to give it a little time, treat it like ... like an adventure."

"There's lots more here that you didn't have back there," her mom added, "like fireflies and ... tree-covered hills and—"

"Aiiiiii!" Erin's scream sliced through Dr. Mac's dreamy

landscape. Something with antennae and long, hairy back legs had just hopped onto Erin's arm. She scooted across the floor in full reverse until she banged her head on the windowsill. That caused the window to slide closed with a bang, which in turn brought three other windows crashing down: *Bang! Bang! Bang!*

Stunned by the shooting-gallery sound effects, no one moved ... except for Michael, who was already lunging for the misguided insect. "I got it!" he cried, but missed.

"No, you don't," Beamer said, jumping in for the kill. "He's mine!" He scrambled after it on hands and knees, scattering boxes everywhere in his wake.

"Beamer!" his mother cried as she lurched to her feet and saved a box of teacups from a shattering experience. "Stop, Beamer!" she called again, grabbing hold of him by his belt loop. "It's a cricket!"

"Mo-o-o-o-ommm," he protested, "it'll get away!"

"That's exactly what I have in mind," she said, planting Beamer and the box of teacups at the same time. Then, as smooth as honey, she glided into the corner and caught the cricket, cupping it gently in her hand. "You can't kill a cricket the first night in a new home," she said, carrying it toward the kitchen. "It would bring terrible luck."

"Bad luck?" Erin complained. "What do you call what happened to my head?"

"Since when are you so superstitious, honey?" Mr. Mac asked with a grin.

"Oh, it's just that crickets don't do anything but good," she answered, peeking into her hand. "They eat parasites and fill the night with singing, that's all."

Beamer rolled his eyes. *Only Mom could get misty-eyed about a bug.*

"The song of the cricket is supposed to guarantee a happy home," she added with a grin to her husband as he opened the door for them to disappear into the kitchen.

Still holding her head, Erin pushed one-handed to her feet. "Maybe that's why it's *not* singing," Erin yelled, following her parents out.

Reaching the door at the same time, Beamer called through it, "It doesn't have to move in with us, does it?"

His mother stepped down into the covered back porch off the kitchen. "Oh, no," she said with a laugh, "The great outdoors will do just fine." She opened the screen door and gently dumped the bewildered cricket onto the step. "Into the backyard with you," she said. "Go."

"That reminds me," said Mr. Mac, pivoting around on his heel to face his kids. "I've been holding out a surprise for you all ... uh, y'all, I mean."

"Surprise?!" The three kids tuned in at the same time.

"It's out back. Just follow the cricket."

"Coming through," Michael yelled, diving toward the door headfirst.

The two boys flew out in a whirlwind. Erin, with slightly more dignity, was close behind.

Their eyes scanned the terrain like radar. It was just after sunset, and a crescent moon hung high in the sky. It had indeed rained that afternoon and the leaves were still dripping—*tap, tap, tap*—and glistening in the moonlight.

All they saw, however, was a couple of large trees ... or was it one tree? It was hard to tell. Two tree trunks were growing out from the same spot, making the shape of a *V*. The *V* was bent on one side where one trunk leaned so close to the ground you could almost run up it—no hands. The trunk straightened up after it crossed over the fence into the next yard.

"Hey, I don't see anything!" Michael complained.

"Take a look up that twisted old tree. It's pretty high up, so you may have to shift around to see it."

Beamer and Michael craned their necks. The sky had cleared since the shower, but the wind was rising again. Insects chirped and buzzed all around them.

Yikes!! It isn't civilized to have so much wildlife right where people lived.

Michael scampered around, peering between the leaves.

"I see it!" Michael yelled.

"Where?" Beamer cried as he ran over to look up.

Then he saw it—a long, dark shadow across one horn of the crescent moon.

*   *   *   *   *

"A tree house!!" Beamer exclaimed, angrily pounding his fist into his pillow. Maybe if it had been digital, had a supercharged video card and network connection, that would have been something else. But a shack in a tree?!

Beamer had stormed back into the house, complaining about the "stupid tree house," the "stupid yard," the "stupid house," and every other "stupid" thing about the "stupid move." The next thing he knew he was marching up the "stupid" stairs early to his "stupid" bed.

Beamer groaned and rolled over. *If it's like everything else around here, that tree house is probably close to falling out of the tree anyway.*

Okay, so his dad had lost his job. No big deal. It was sort of a thing that happened in Southern California. Half the dads in his Scout troop had lost their jobs before it happened to his dad. So why'd they have to move? And, of all places, why here in Middle America?

Beamer slid his pillow over to escape the light from the street lamps. It was just his luck that one of the few working street lamps on Murphy Street was right in front of his house. With no curtains on his two front windows, that was liable to be a problem for awhile. It occurred to him that a well-thrown rock could take care of it. Unfortunately, he was a Christian kid, and they didn't do that sort of thing.

Sounds picked at his ears—a distant siren, the rumbling of a heavy truck, the hiss of tires on wet pavement. McCauley Boulevard, one of the city's main drags, was only half a block away. He found himself wishing for the freeway back home, with its soothing eight-lane rumble. It always made him think of the surf.

What he didn't hear was what his mom said he *should* be hearing—crickets. Oh, he heard buzzing and chirping, but it wasn't from crickets. That much he knew from visiting his grandparents in Kentucky.

"Man!" he groaned. "Even Mother Nature doesn't work right around here!"

Suddenly, just over the roof of the house next door, Beamer saw a light flash toward the horizon. *A meteor!* Without thinking, he made a wish, licked his thumb and squashed it with a twist into the palm of his other hand.

Beamer was too cool to do stuff like making wishes when anyone was around. But he believed in wishes. He figured God listened to wishes as much as he did to prayers, at least from kids. Of course, Beamer prayed too. But right now, he needed all the help he could get. And if a "falling star" could help get him home, who was he to quibble?

4
Planet Murphy Street

For the next few days, Beamer wouldn't even look into the backyard, let alone the tree house. Xbox controllers and Lego confabs were his thing.

Erin wasn't taking the move any better than Beamer. So far, all expeditions into the city had failed to reveal a single decent-sized mall. Not that she'd been out that much. After all, washing and drying her hair took most of her time.

Beamer figured if the air conditioner didn't come soon, she'd probably go bald, after which she'd go crazy and they'd have to lock her up in the attic with the web and cover the noise of her unearthly shrieks by playing loud music. That's when the neighbors would start picketing the house ... until they'd be forced to move back home. Pretty neat scenario!

At the moment, though, nobody was allowed in the attic except for bug scientists and engineers who were bringing in enough chemical and electronic equipment

to find E.T. Traffic through the house was up there with rush hour on the freeway, much to his mother's frustration. In the meantime, with all the zaps, hisses, and bubbling sounds above his bedroom ceiling, Beamer's latest Lego masterpiece was beginning to look like a sci-fi creature feature. He couldn't really understand their high-tech muttering, but, so far, they hadn't found the mutant arachnid who built that web metropolis.

Finally, Beamer's mom kicked her juvenile hermit out of the house. There he was, face-to-face (or knee to pavement) with Murphy Street. Actually, it wasn't much of a street — only one block long. The houses on Murphy Street were large by Shadow Beach Lane standards, and most had something strange about them, like the one that had a garden on the roof—flowers, bushes, trees—the whole plant kingdom. One side of another house was built into the trunk of a humongous tree—a live tree! There was also a house with rows of high, narrow windows and tons of carved wood and stone and glass. Beamer gagged when he saw it. It was so ... pink!

A high brick wall ran behind all the houses on the other side of Murphy Street. And on the other side of that wall was "the park"—Michael's park.

"Gotcha!" the little know-it-all bragged to Beamer. They were on their bikes, looking through the small park gate on Parkview Court. Since Parkview crossed the northern end of Murphy Street, the park was, in fact, just around the corner.

"All right, so there's a park," Beamer grumbled. "Big deal! Every city's got parks." He had to admit, though, that this one *did* look big. He couldn't even see the other side. "So, where's the zoo?" he asked with a cynical smirk.

"That-a-way," Michael answered triumphantly, pointing off to his left. There, about a football-field-length away, was a large gate shaped like two elephants standing on their hind legs. Michael was definitely on a roll in the I-told-you-so department.

"See that?" Michael said, pointing a different direction.

"Yeah," Beamer shrugged as he looked beyond a picnic area and a baseball field to a wide range of tall trees.

"That's where the dinosaurs live," Michael announced knowingly.

"What dinosaurs?" Beamer gave him the standard big brother put-down.

"The ones that make the cracks in the sidewalk over on Murphy Street."

"Ri-i-i-g-g-h-t," Beamer drawled out of the corner of his mouth. "Dinosaurs are extinct."

"That's just it. They're not!" Michael jumped back in. "They were just shy around people, so they went and hid. That forest has places that haven't even been explored yet! I'll bet they come out to hunt on Murphy Street at night."

"Yeah ... sure," Beamer muttered, peering into the dark depths of the woods. Secretly, he thought the idea sounded promising. After all, he'd never seen cracks in the streets back home.

Near sunset Beamer was skateboarding around the fire hydrants and lampposts along Murphy Street when a jagged slash of lighting jolted him nearly off his board. It had started a couple of hours ago. "Heat lightning" is what his mom had told him it was, but it sounded just the same as the normal kind, and something about it happening in a clear sky made it all the more spooky. Lights were beginning to come on up and down the street.

The biggest house on Murphy Street, however, was still dark, except for the tower. A large shadow stood in the third-story tower window, peering out at the street. Since Beamer was the only thing in the street at the moment, it gave him a particularly eerie feeling.

Another flash ripped open the darkening sky, followed quickly by a deafening *Kaboom ... Shreee*! Beamer looked up in time to see lightning sizzling down the lightning rod on the big house like it was being sucked up. The tower lights immediately blipped out. Beamer skidded to a stop to take a closer look.

People called it Parker's Castle. With turrets on each corner and a tower in the middle, it looked like a transplant from Transylvania.

Right now, though, it was a dark hole in the block, its windows looking like dark eyes in a dead body. Suddenly the lights came back on, not just a few as before, but all of them, like a giant Christmas tree. *Somebody must have gone through the house, flipping light switches while the electricity was off.* The startled Beamer tripped off his board, which shot out from under him like a cruise missile.

Beamer chased it down the street and jumped on it just before it got to his house. By the time he slammed the Ma-cIntyre front door behind him, his lungs were nearly bursting from the effort.

Then his mother said something even more frightening—"To the showers, everyone! School tomorrow!"

The very thought sent Beamer searching for his mom's credit card. A plane ticket home, a corner in a boxcar, slave quarters in a riverboat—he'd have taken anything to avoid P.E. in a new school.

Suicide—that's what it would be ... him against the natives—seven hundred middle-schoolers all anxious to push his buttons. A personal force field was what he needed, or, failing that, a deep gulp of laughing gas. Unfortunately, he was fresh out of both.

*   *   *   *   *

Lacking an invisibility cloak, Beamer tried to look as inconspicuous as possible that first day. It worked ... until he opened his mouth. All he said was "I'm Beamer MacIntyre," and everybody started giggling. It was like he'd just dropped in from Neptune. He couldn't believe it. *Those turkeys think I'm the one who talks funny! They're the ones who pronounce words like they're wrapped around inner tubes.*

Then the sky fell in. It happened during recess, right after a disgusting ravioli lunch. Figuring that basketball hoops, a place on a kickball team, and balls in general would be hard to come by, especially for a new kid, Beamer had brought his own bat and tether baseball. A little batting practice couldn't hurt, and it would be a heck of a lot more fun than waiting in line.

Finding an out-of-the-way spot, he drove a stake with the attached tether baseball into the ground. After a few early misses, Beamer started getting his old ball-slugging form back. Unfortunately, he failed to notice another kind of slugging behind a nearby row of bushes.

Three overgrown eighth graders had a very skinny seventh grader backpedaling full throttle.

"So, where's your money, huh?" a Hulk clone demanded as he jabbed a muscle-bound finger into the smaller kid's chest.

"Yeah, Ghoulie," a second boy sneered, giving him another poke, "a rich dude like you—come on now—what's the problem? Where is it?"

"I ... I forgot," the trembling boy said, faltering back with each poke. A few more pokes and the kid would be limited to a career as Swiss cheese.

Mr. Big Cheese grabbed him by his shirt. "You forgot?! Not very smart for a nerd," he snarled. He yanked the boy off the ground by his shirt, swung him around, and dropped him to the ground like a bag of elbows and knees. "What did I say would happen," the bully continued, "if—"

He didn't get to finish. Beamer didn't mean to do it. Actually he just missed the tetherball when it jerked back toward him after a hard smack. It zipped past Beamer's out-stretched hand and straight into the chin of the smallest goon. It bounced from chin to knee to forehead around the rest of them like a pinball before it wrapped—Wha-Wha-Wha-Wha-Wha-WHAPP!—around the leader's chest and arms.

"Argghhh!" the suddenly-mummified bully shrieked.

Wasting no time to figure out what was happening, Ghoulie took advantage of the confusion and shot out of there like a spit wad.

For Beamer, though, there was no escape, and one look at the converging circle of goons suggested he had come to a major moment in his life—like maybe the *last* moment in his life.

5

Goons, Geeks, and Other Life Forms

"Hey, look, I'm sorry," Beamer stammered as two kids carried him by the elbows over to the teen mummy. Kids all around were snickering and giggling. The bully's head whirled around with a vengeance and immediately the pockets of laughter choked off. "I ... I didn't see you," Beamer said anxiously, fumbling to unwind the tether wrapping.

Then the big kid burst out of the remaining strands like a cartoon hand grenade exploding, sending the ball careening off the chin of one of his yokels.

"You dolt," he growled, grabbing Beamer by the shirt collar. Two of Beamer's buttons popped off in a trajectory that took them right across his nose. "Are you ready to die?"

"Who? Me?" Beamer squeaked, feeling like a chicken about to get his neck wrung. "It was an accident." Actually, with his throat crushed to the size of a toothpick, what actually came out was "Oooo? mmmmeee? Iiik aaaahs an aaaxcccnnn."

"Look, nobody gets away with making Jared Foster look bad," the guy with the vice grip hissed. "Nobody!! Do you understand?"

"Sh ... shh ... sure," Beamer gurgled, his only air supply coming from the bully's hot ravioli breath. Any closer to ter-minato-kid's flared nostrils and Beamer could have checked out his sinuses.

"You've got a few things to learn" snarled Jared, suddenly pushing Beamer away. Then, before Beamer could remember how to breathe, a bulging finger jerked in front of his nose. "One!" Jared growled. "You don't get in my way. Two ..." A second finger snapped up next to the first. Beamer's eyes crossed, trying to focus on them. "I run the local charity. And, as of today, you're my biggest contributor!"

"Con-tri-bu-t ...?" Beamer squeaked, his voice box not yet thoroughly decompressed.

"Money, stupid," one of the other goons explained.

"You give two dollars to 'The Fund,'" said Jared, "and everybody gets taken care of."

"Two!" Beamer gasped. "But I don't need taking care of."

"You will, dude, if you don't pay," the shortest of the gang members promised, giving him a twisted grin.

"What Slocum means," added the leader in a suddenly formal voice, "is that the Fund is how we take care of kids ... uh ... less fortunate than us."

"That's right," said an adult who suddenly appeared next to Jared. "Hi! You must be new," she said, looking at the still-pale Beamer.

He recognized her as the "yard duty" volunteer.

"You know," the smiling lady continued, "with many kids around here having trouble just getting milk money, Jared's idea has been a godsend. I know you'll be proud to be part of it." She gave Beamer's tormentor a friendly pat on the shoulder and walked off.

Beamer tried to wander off too, but Jared smacked him to attention with a backhanded blow to the chest. "Oh, and another thing," he said in a hushed voice, "watch who you choose for friends."

No sooner had Beamer gotten his breath back than he heard, "Don't forget: two bucks ... tomorrow!" Jared was looking back at him over his shoulder, pointing his finger like a pistol, "or it's '*Hasta la vista* to you, baby.'"

Beamer finally drew his first decent breath. Every kid within fifty feet was staring at him. Tucking his hands in his pockets, he tried to whistle, but he sounded more like a sputtering teapot. Thankfully, his audience began to melt away.

Great! Beamer groaned to himself. *My first day in school and I'm already public enemy number one to the school's number-one public enemy.*

*   *   *   *   *

Money ... money ... money was all that Beamer could think of as he walked home that afternoon. Maybe he could bring in a little cash by making a deal not to show his sister's naked baby pictures to the ninth-grade drill team. Unfortunately, with Dad out of work so long, the idea of an "allowance" was ancient history.

As he turned to walk up his driveway, Beamer noticed a squirrel next to the backyard fence. It had something shiny in its mouth. *Hey, maybe the little rodent had found a gold ring or a diamond or something.* He quietly dropped his backpack and crept slowly toward it. Suddenly he crunched a puddle of leaves. The squirrel darted across the yard and up the bent trunk of the tree. Beamer dashed after it and ran halfway up the trunk before the little pipsqueak disappeared between two leafy branches.

Beamer sighed and leaned against a branch. He could barely see the tree house far above. It looked like a banana with outriggers ... or something else. He couldn't quite put his finger on it. But, then, of course, he didn't care.

No sooner had he slid back down to the ground than he heard a chittering sound. Looking back up the tree, he saw the squirrel again, chattering away like Aunt Bertha on Thanksgiving. Beamer started to walk away, but right when he thought he had a grip on reality, the squirrel's noises started to make sense!

"Hey, brick foot!" the squirrel said in a high-pitched chirp. "Get those nut-crunchers off my turf!"

"What?" yelped Beamer, looking down at his feet, then back up in surprise.

"My acorns, you lunk head! You're trompin' all over 'em!" the squirrel chattered louder in a decidedly Southern accent. The squirrel suddenly disappeared again between the branches.

"Hey! Wait!" Beamer said, climbing hands and feet like a kid going the wrong way up a playground slide. "How come you can talk?"

"Squirrels only!" the little rodent ordered as it stuck its head out of a hollow in the tree—probably where it hid its hoard of nuts. "Didn't you read the sign?" Then it giggled.

"Sign?" Beamer questioned, looking around. *Hey, since when do squirrels giggle? Okay, maybe Chip and Dale, but they're chipmunks, not squirrels, and cartoons on top of that.*

Suddenly the giggles broke into laughter and out from

behind the branches peeked a girl. "Had ya goin', didn't I?" she chortled.

At least Beamer *thought* it was a girl. The jeans, camouflage shirt, and four-barrel, super-charged squirt gun slung across her back didn't help. Then she turned her head and there was a dishwater-blonde ponytail. Of course that wasn't a sure sign, but it was a start.

"The squirrel and I are old friends," she said. "His family's lived in this here tree forever." She stretched out her words in a drawl wide enough for *Gone with the Wind.*

Beamer climbed toward her. "What are you doing in my tree, anyway?"

"Your tree? Part of it hangs over *my* yard, ya' know." She pointed to a second floor window in the house next door. "That's my room up there."

Beamer looked around. Sure enough, he was standing where the bent trunk hung over the next yard. "Well, so what?" he shrugged. "The tree is *planted* in *my* yard and no court in the country would say this is *your* tree." He looked up at the tree house. "And if you've been messin' up my tree house, you're in a lot of trouble."

"Hah! That shows how much *you* know! It's not a tree house!"

6

Spaceships Don't Grow on Trees

"What are you talkin' about?" Beamer said, rolling his eyes. "Of course it's a—"

"It's a spaceship!" she trumpeted.

"A what?" Beamer stammered with a stunned look. He peered up through the branches like he was trying to use X-ray vision.

Of course! Why didn't I see it before—the bullet shape, flattened out some—broader than it is high. The ship's nose was tilted down slightly, as if it had crashed into the tree.

"If you'd cared the tiniest bit," the girl chided him, "you'd have known."

But he could barely hear her now. There was something—no more than a speck—way out in space. All of a sudden, it was like he could see ... forever.

The next thing he knew he was inside it, looking out the window.

A lower half of a huge ball with rings around it loomed before his eyes. It's the planet Saturn. The spaceship is doing the loop the loop around Saturn!

Bad move. Every star pilot from Rigel to Betelgeuse has heard of the rings. Forget the exploded moon dust theory and the ice cube ring-around-the-planet idea.

Where did that come from? Beamer thought. *What made me think I knew that?*

The truth is that the rings are an infamous graveyard of spaceships, which makes Saturn one major tombstone. For a million years, interstellar voyagers have been trapped in the giant planet's super-cool, freeze-your-buns electromagnetic whirlpool.

Of course, at first nobody knows it is a trap. They just think it is the ride of their lives, whirling around that multicolored ball, playing big-time dodgeball with all the pretty rocks that make up the rings. Only too late do they discover that they are doomed to become one of those shiny chunks. Yes, by the time they figure out there is no exit to this ride, their spaceships will be halfway cocooned in a kind of sticky gook.

What am I doing here? For that matter, who's talking in my head?

This time is lucky, though. One of those gooey rocks nicked the ship — actually splattered was more like it, exploding into something between fireworks and a huge geyser of multicolored paint. The ship recoiled, spinning away from the rings, end over end.

Inside the ship, Beamer was also spinning end over end. By the time his head cleared, the monster-planet Jupiter was outside his window. Unfortunately, the giant red spot in the middle of the planet seems to have taken a liking to the little rocket and it's trying to suck it up like a Popsicle. It's a tussle to escape the big planet's puckered, red lips, but a little backfire from the rockets and those lips spit us back out into the cosmos.

Scenes change quickly. Now we're shooting the asteroid belt like a pinball. Shields on full, we bounce off those little planetoids as if they are made of rubber. Even so, the ship doesn't take it too well. Gravity control is going haywire and everybody and everything is bouncing around.

Somewhere this side of Mars, something really goes wrong. The sensors fail to detect a passing comet. It whirls the ship around like a carnival ride and flings it toward a small blue and white planet — the third one from the star.

"Hey! Are you listening to me?" a voice piped in. "What are you doing, anyway?"

"Huh?" Beamer mumbled, shaking his head to clear his vision. *Wow! I've had some hare-brained fantasies in my time, but this one—*

"Nothing," he said. "Go on. What were you ... uhm ... saying?"

"I was saying that it's haunted!"

"Haunted? What is?" Beamer asked, thinking about the big house down the street.

"The tree ship!" the girl repeated impatiently. "What's the matter with your ears?"

Beamer sat in stunned silence. Haunted cemeteries, haunted houses he could understand, but haunted spaceships ... and in trees, no less. "That's ridiculous!"

"Good grief! Don't you know anything?" she scolded him. She started to shinny along a branch toward him. "It's practically a legend!"

"Legends are for Indian mounds, foggy castles, and other ancient-type stuff," Beamer cried impatiently. "Not tree houses!"

"Well, it's practically ancient," she insisted, hanging upside down in front of him like a tree sloth. "It's been here as long as anybody can remember."

"So what does the haunting? A ghost made out of leaves?" Beamer said with a smirk.

The girl straddled a branch above him. "Well, there's one way to find out, kid."

"Beamer, the name's Beamer!" he retorted. "Beamer MacIntyre. And I want nothing to do with that thing, haunted or not—nothing to do with this house, this block, or anybody livin' on it. And the last thing I need is a girl who thinks she's a commando and talks about haunted tree houses!"

"Oooooh ... major attitude problem," she taunted him. "Seein' how ya' rescued Ghoulie today, I expected better."

She swung to the lowest branch and dangled in the air a moment before dropping to the ground. Whether or not she was a girl, Beamer was pretty sure she was half monkey.

"Incidentally, my name's Scilla—Scilla Bruzelski. And just you try and keep me outta *my* tree!" she yelled up at him as she huffed and strode like a peacock through her back door.

Beamer heard the screen door slam behind her. He wasn't proud of the way he'd just acted, but he was too busy feeling sorry for himself to worry about anyone else. After all, besides leaving his old friends, having the local creepazoid on his case, being hero to a nerd, and being condemned to live on a prehistoric street, how many things could go wrong in one lifetime?

An insect landed on his hand. "Yipe!" he yelped, flinging it off. It landed on a branch nearby. He raised his foot for the death squish, and then remembered his mom's words. "Oh, a cricket!" He crawled over for a closer look. It was such a pale green that it was almost white. It turned and faced him as if it was sizing him up, then suddenly sprang away.

Beamer was usually pretty much the Terminator where bugs were concerned, but it didn't seem right to kill one that was supposed to sing. Of course, the crickets around here didn't appear to sing at all, as far as he could tell. *Maybe they all have laryngitis or something.*

*   *   *   *   *

Beamer thought he had it knocked the next day. Good ol' Mom came through with the milk money. After all, it was for a good cause—sort of. Before the first bell, Beamer headed straight for Jared in playground central. As confident as a mouse about to snatch cheese from a mousetrap, he dug into his pocket and pulled out a wad of crisp bills.

Luckily Jared never heard the vacuum-powered gasp behind him. Like the dutiful, trustworthy Scout he was, Beamer had put his mom's money into his bank. The only trouble was that was where he'd also kept his old play money. Yep, you guessed it. He was standing within spitting distance of Jared holding a fistful of worthless colored paper!

As luck would have it, Jared chose that moment to turn around. Fortunately, or maybe thanks to a little angel dust, somebody opened the restroom door smack in front of Beamer's face. And Jared stepped inside without even seeing him.

It was time for plan "B," otherwise known as cold, sweaty panic! When that didn't work, he opted for plan "C," which was to lay low. It wasn't particularly cool stopping to peek around every corner and through the hinges of every door. But it was either that or face the Matter Disintegrator—Jared's fists.

The hardest times were lunch and recess. Once, Beamer had to hide inside a playground slide tube. Luckily, by the time the next kid slid down and bumped him out of the tube, Jared's warp-brain goon was gone.

Five minutes after the final bell, however, Beamer's luck ran out.

7

Life in the Toilet

Beamer was in the bathroom when he heard the door open and Jared's laugh. One heartbeat later, Beamer was hiding in the handicapped stall, perched on top of the toilet seat.

"Yeah," Slocum bragged, "that Henderson guy took one look at this fist and emptied his pockets into my hand." He laughed like a hyena.

"Slocum, you taken care of the seventh graders?" asked Jeffries.

"Most of 'em," Slocum answered. "Haven't seen that new kid though. Hey, I heard he's the dork who moved into that place on Murphy Street."

"D'ya mean the one with—" Jared started.

"I'd like to be there when he tries climbing up to it," Jeffries chortled.

"In the meantime, find him," Jared ordered. "If he's not out sick, he's gonna be."

"Yeah," Slocum added with another hyena laugh, "he looked pretty sick after our little talk on Monday."

"My nose is bleedin'!" Jared yelped suddenly. "Jeffries, get me some toilet paper, quick!"

The boy bolted for one of the stalls. Unfortunately, it was the one where Beamer was hiding.

It's amazing how many things can go through your mind when you're a split second away from total annihilation. Beamer saw the latch turn. There was no place to go! Soon he would be history. No, he wasn't old enough for history—the evening paper, maybe. It'd be kind of a short obituary. He hoped his mom wouldn't give them his sixth-grade picture. *The toilet—what a way to go.*

The door swung open. Beamer, who at the last second had leaped onto the door coat hook, was slammed into the stall wall. "Oof!" he gasped, the blow knocking the air out of him. Jeffries ripped off the paper in a flash and was back outside, never noticing the kid hanging there like a side of beef. Beamer sighed in relief and stepped back onto the seat.

"Here you go, dude," Jeffries said, handing the paper to Jared.

Jared stuffed it up his nose and tilted his head back. "Hey, get some more and put some cold water on it."

Beamer braced himself and leaped back on the coat hook as the steps approached.

"No, you jerk!" Jared ordered, "a paper towel this time. That other stuff falls apart."

The footsteps changed direction and Beamer sighed in relief. He heard water from the faucet.

Jared dabbed at his nose a minute, then turned around. "How's it look, Slocum?"

"Pretty good," he said, looking up Jared's nostril as if it were a periscope. "I think it's stopped."

"Ya *think* so?" Jared flared. "I don't need *thinking*. I don't want nobody to think somebody got to me. Come on," he said to his minions. He tossed the crumpled paper towel over his shoulder and walked out. The paper wad arched over the stall door and bounced off Beamer's head. When Beamer finally heard the door shut, he let his breath out and slid to the floor like melting candle wax.

* * * * *

Beamer picked up Michael from the nearby after-school daycare center, and they set off toward home along one of many beaten paths through the park. While Michael chattered away about the social ills of the fourth grade, Beamer kept an eye out for Jared and company. They came out into a broad clearing. For awhile they were able to hug close to the tree line. Finally, though, the forest twisted right and the way home meant that they had to launch out across the clearing.

"Wait a minute," Beamer said, stopping to make one last check.

"What for?" Michael asked.

"Nothin'." Beamer finished his survey. "Okay, let's go."

Then, less than fifty steps into the clearing, they heard a shrill screech. Beamer's head whipped around. A boy erupted from another forest path about half a football field away. The long, skinny legs that knocked with each stride told Beamer it was probably Ghoulie. He was running full tilt, school papers streaming out behind him like confetti.

A moment later three other boys blew out of the same opening in hot pursuit.

Beamer's eyes popped wide. It was Jared and his clones out for the kill. "Run, Michael!" Beamer shouted to his brother, pushing him ahead.

"Hey!" Michael protested. "Stop shovin' ..."

"Move it! I haven't got time to argue. It's life and death!!"

They broke into a run as Ghoulie streaked by. "What happened?" Beamer yelled.

"I lost my contribution," he said between gasps.

"Okay, *he's* in trouble," said Michael, breathing heavily. "So why are *we* running?"

"Because if those guys recognize me, you'll be a witness to my execution and dead meat too."

Michael's stubby legs shifted into overdrive. A moment later the fugitive trio plunged into the middle of a football game, turning a long punt return into a messy four-way fumble. Shouts and shrieks erupted on every side.

There was no time for "Sorrys." For that matter, Jared's troops were already giving the football team an instant re-play.

Dead ahead was the park's museum surrounded by flowers and hedges. With no time for a detour, the threesome launched like awkward hurdlers over the first hedge. More of Ghoulie's papers fluttered away. Two hedges later Michael took a tumble. Beamer skidded to a halt and yanked him back up.

All three were exactly in step for the fifth hedgerow. Unfortunately, a trio of very proper middle-aged ladies stepped through a rosebush arbor right in front of them. It was not a pretty sight. The boys mowed them down like corn-stalks. Actually, they didn't touch them, but the surprise was enough. The ladies recoiled—one of them backward over a side hedge, another into a bed of pansies, while the third splashed into a fountain pool.

Beamer looked behind to see Jared's head pop into view as he cleared the first hedge. With one hedge to go, the timed sprinkler system came to their rescue.

There was a yelp, and then—Phzzz! Plopp! Splatt!—their pursuers landed in a muddy skid, splattering even more yuck over the poor women.

By the time Jared's mud wamps wrestled their way out of the bog, Beamer and his crew had gained several precious seconds.

As the seventh-grade brain trust, Ghoulie quickly calculated speed, trajectory, and the distance home, factoring in approximate leg length and muscle development. He concluded, "We don't have a chance!"

To their left was the brick wall that skirted the side of the park. Murphy Street was the next block over, but to get there they had to go around the wall by way of the gate on Parkview Court.

Just then they heard a shout. It was Scilla scampering on an intercept course. "Hey! Y'all follow me!" she shouted, cocking her head toward the wall.

"Where?" Beamer gasped between gulps of breath as they veered after her.

"Just trust me," she fired back at him.

That was easier said than done. Jared's attack force was bearing down on them. And where was Scilla leading them? Straight into a ten-foot-high wall!

Winding through a maze of trees and bushes, Scilla suddenly dived between two humongous flowering bushes. Brushing leaves and flower petals from their eyes, her three followers found themselves staring at the wall. This was *not* a good moment.

"Great!" Beamer exclaimed. "Do you supply the firing squad too?"

"Keep your pants on," she shot back at him. She slid aside a slab of plywood so covered with glued-down rocks and dirt and weeds that it looked like part of the ground.

"A hole!" Ghoulie exclaimed.

"A *dark* hole!" Michael added with a gulp.

"Get in there, quick," she ordered, shoving him into the hole.

"Hey!" he protested. "What about spiders? And Mom'll kill me if I get my school clothes dirty."

"Jared will kill you if you don't!"

He dropped in and was gone.

"Yo! Geek patrol!" Jared shouted from nearby, as he thrashed through the bushes looking for them. "Come out now and maybe I won't turn you into chopped beef."

Scilla and Beamer scurried into the hole behind Ghoulie like frightened groundhogs. Not half a breath after Scilla dragged the plywood back over the hole, Jared's head poked through the bushes to see ... nothing.

Meanwhile the fugitives found themselves climbing down a long ladder.

"A detour through the center of the earth wasn't exactly what I had in mind," grumbled Beamer. Suddenly a tiny light flashed in front of his eyes; then another; then a hundred. His feet stumbled onto the floor and he whirled around in bewilderment. There were lights ... everywhere!

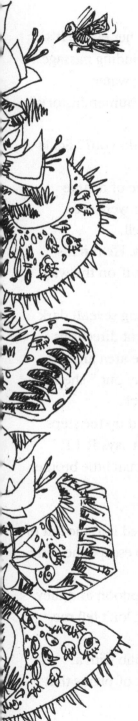

8

The Haunting of Murphy Street

Beamer had been in caves before, but never in one that was lit up like Christmas.

"What is this, firefly city?" exclaimed Ghoulie, his eyes reflecting a thousand tiny lights flickering on and off.

"Wow!" chirped Michael as he jumped about trying to catch one.

"You haven't seen nothin' yet," Scilla said as she removed an old-fashioned lamp hung on the wall. She turned a knob. There was no flame, but a large bulb suddenly glowed with a kind of liquid.

Michael touched the bulb. "Hey, it's not even warm!"

"Yeah, and the light's the same color as the light from the fireflies," added Ghoulie.

"We can figure out this stuff later; let's just get out of here," said Beamer, looking around nervously. "You're sure there's a way out, aren't you?"

"Of course, you ninny," said Scilla, rolling her eyes. "It's this way." She led them trudging through a winding passage. They could hear the distant sound of trickling water.

"This has got to be the longest shortcut in human history," grumbled Beamer.

"Yeah, but you don't see Jared anywhere, do you?" Scilla shot back.

The passage opened up into a room the size of a large classroom, only twice as tall. Here the fireflies were even denser and portions of the walls glowed as well.

"Whoa!" gasped Ghoulie at the light show. He ran his fingers across the velvety-textured glowing stuff on the wall. "Seems to be some kind of moss."

"Where do those go?" asked Beamer, eyeing several dark passages that led off from the room in different directions.

"Don't know, but Grandma says the whole area around the park is honeycombed with caves. This way out," she said, leading them to a staircase carved into the rock.

"Hey!" Michael blurted as Scilla scrambled up the steps. "Did you see the letters carved in this rock? It says R.I.P."

"R.I.P.—what?" Beamer asked with his usual little brother put-down.

"Rest in Peace, duh!" Michael retorted.

As the light from Scilla's lantern disappeared into the loft of the staircase, the others scrambled after her to escape the eerie glow of the cave.

A few minutes later Scilla pushed up a trapdoor, and they entered another place with creepy lighting. "Don't tell me, another cave?" Beamer grumbled.

"More biological illumination," said Ghoulie with a whistle. It wasn't fireflies this time but a forest of plants that glowed in the dark.

Beamer lightly knocked on the dark wall. It clinked like glass. "We're in a greenhouse," exclaimed Beamer, "except the windows are all blacked out."

"This way," chimed in Scilla as she led them toward a door at the end of the building.

"Hey, I think I saw that one move," said Beamer. They all gathered around a bush with glowing purple flowers. Suddenly a bird with glowing wings fluttered out of the bush. They all jumped back, screaming at the same time, "*Aiiiii*!!"

Still screaming, Michael ran to the door and flung it open.

"Ouch ... Whoa!" yelped the others who were right behind him, wincing from the sudden assault of sunlight. Then they breathed a sigh of relief ... that is, until their eyes adjusted.

"Just exactly what planet are we on?" gulped Beamer. They were in a garden—but not like any they'd ever seen.

"Nice place," Ghoulie gulped as he scanned the dark spires that loomed over the garden. "If you like sleeping in a casket."

Yep, you guessed it. They were in the backyard of Parker's Castle.

"What's the next stop—the torture chamber?" Beamer rasped at Scilla.

"Keep your shirts on," Scilla barked back at them. "The gate's over here." She started down a path through the garden. "Just don't touch anything!" she added.

Actually Michael had already started touching everything. A plant suddenly snapped at him. "Yipes!" he yelped. "It's a man-eating garden!"

"Keep your hands to yourself," Scilla repeated. "This isn't your everyday garden."

"You don't say," mocked Beamer.

Actually, it would have been beautiful if it hadn't also been so weird. Many of the plants seemed right out of *The Wizard of Oz*. There were flowers the size of a bicycle wheel, giant orchids, and walls of flowering vines. Huge and bright, they seemed to move from more than the wind. There was, however, no yellow brick road.

"Grandma says this house was here even before Murphy Street," said Scilla.

"How can you have a house without a street?" asked Michael.

"A hundred years ago, this whole area was a big estate—the park too."

"What's an estate?" Michael asked.

"It's like a fancy farm," Scilla explained.

"What do you suppose happened to the people who ate what they farmed?" muttered Michael, jumping back from a yellow flower that spit red dust at him.

Beamer suddenly tripped over a water hose into a wall of vines. The next thing he knew, the vine was crawling all over him, wrapping him up like a spider in a web. "*Aiiiii!*" he yelled. "Somebody get me out of this!"

Ghoulie jumped after him but only succeeded in getting himself in the same mess. They both yelped and writhed in full panic mode.

Scilla rushed to them, shouting in a whisper, "Quiet! You'll get Old Lady Parker after us!" At the same time she grabbed a spray bottle that was sitting on a little stand and sprayed the plant. Immediately it shrank back. Another spray sent it into full retreat, unwinding its tendrils from the flailing, now quietly screaming, boys.

"Pipe down, you two!" Scilla whispered loudly. "She's left

little bottles of plant repellent all over the place and, anyway, it wasn't going to eat you."

"Just wanted a little snuggle, huh," sputtered Beamer. "And we were supposed to know this *how??*" *"Boy Eaten by Killer Bush"—some obituary that would make!*

Around one more bend in the cobblestone road they came to the gate. It was big and heavy, made of black iron rods all twisted into fancy shapes. Beamer warily eyed a design at the top. It looked something like a dragon diving out of the sky.

"The lock's been broken for years," Scilla said as she triggered the handle. "They've never bothered to fix it. Most people wouldn't be caught dead in Old Lady Parker's yard anyway."

"That's probably because there's a nine in ten chance that's exactly how they'd be caught—dead!" quipped Beamer.

A moment later they were running across Ms. Parker's front lawn, heading lickety-split toward Murphy Street.

"Made it!/Whew!/Thank you, God!" they all exclaimed in a collective sigh of relief that probably altered the air patterns around Middleton.

"No thanks to you!" Beamer snapped at Ghoulie, throwing his backpack to the ground. "You led them right to me!"

"Hey, I was just running," Ghoulie shot back. "I didn't have time to check the traffic report."

"Well, next time find somebody besides me to save your behind."

"The way I see it, she's the one that saved both our behinds," Ghoulie countered, pointing at Scilla.

"Yeah, if you don't count all the narrow escapes along the way!" he shot back at him. Beamer spun around and strutted off red-faced toward his house, pulling Michael by the hand.

"Hey," Ghoulie called to Scilla, "can I use your phone to call home? If I'm not home on time, my nanny starts calling the National Guard."

"You've got a nanny?" Scilla asked.

"Yeah, my parents don't get home until late."

"Well," Scilla said, looking up toward the house, "Grandma's not home right now, and I'm not allowed to have any of y'all in the house when she's not."

"Come on," Beamer called from his porch. "You can use mine."

"Better watch it, though," Scilla said out of the side of her mouth. "His place is haunted." She laughed and skipped away into her house.

Ghoulie hesitated, eyeing Beamer's house suspiciously.

Moments later he was looking up and around the entryway, checking every nook and cranny for some sign of an "ecto-plasmic manifestation." He'd heard somebody say that in a movie somewhere. It had something to do with gooey, slimy, glowing stuff that was a sign that ghosts were nearby.

Then he heard an eerie, high-pitched voice coming from the living room. "Mama, you've got to say *something* about me. Am I ... am I ...?"

Ghoulie's eyes grew wide when he peered through the hallway door. A large bug-shaped, one-eyed creature, growling in a high pitch, was careening across the living room, heading right toward him.

9

Double, Double, Toil, and Trouble

Ghoulie dived behind a couch, but not before the bug grabbed his pants leg. "*Aiiiii!*" he yelped, clutching his pants tightly to keep them from being sucked into the beast.

A woman dashed up behind the bug. She glanced at a manual in her hand and shouted, "Gopher, wait. I mean, Gophah, waaeet." The creature suddenly stopped. She sighed and wiped the hair from in front of her eyes. "Gopher ... uh ... Gopha sahleep," she pronounced carefully. The object obediently scooted across the floor into an opening in the wall which immediately snapped shut.

Haunted doesn't begin to describe this place, thought Ghoulie as he pulled up his pants and tightened his belt.

"Can't you keep that thing locked up?" a man asked in frustration.

"I'm trying," the woman answered, "but it

automatically leaps to life and starts vacuuming away whenever it detects a higher-than-normal particle content in the carpet. And with all the scientists and tech crews tramping through this house, the particle content is way up there."

"We'd lived here a week before Mom found that manual," Beamer said as he suddenly appeared next to Ghoulie. "Everything works by voice command around here."

"Emily, you make me tired." It was the squeaky voice again, now in a slightly lower-pitch.

Ghoulie stared at the man who was reading aloud in that weird voice and pacing mechanically across the floor. *How could Beamer seem so normal with a father like that?*

"That's just Dad getting ready for tonight's play rehearsal at the university," Beamer said. "He's a Professor who directs plays. Right now he's trying to figure out how all the characters will move around on stage, so he's reading everybody's lines. The phone's over here," he added in a whisper. "Dad just goes a little nuts when he gets to play all the parts himself."

It sounded more like a bad case of multiple personality disorder to Ghoulie. Keeping a wary eye on Beamer's dad, he stood back up and turned to see Michael already at the phone.

"No, Georgie, you can't come over now," Michael said into the receiver. "My mom says there are too many people here already. Besides, it's not our Xbox day, so—"

Ghoulie jumped when Beamer grabbed his arm and tugged him toward the door at the end of the hallway.

"Are you gonna hafta go back to the park for those papers you lost?" Beamer asked.

"No way," Ghoulie replied. "My neck's worth more than a report on *Moby Dick*. Besides, it's on my hard drive—words, pictures, even the sound effects I had attached to it on a CD.

I'll just make another copy."

"Sound effects? That must be some report! What kind of computer have you got?" Beamer asked.

"The works," Ghoulie said with a shrug. "You know, the usual absentee-parent guilt package." The truth was, Ghoulie rarely saw his parents, except at breakfast and right before bedtime. But when it came to games and toys and high-tech wizardry, he had it all.

"Right," Beamer murmured as he pushed through the kitchen door.

Beamer's mother was now leaning over the stove saying, "Stove, plate fo'ah, ahwn, mae-di-uh'm." One of the sections on the seamless stove top began to glow.

"It took Mom half a day to figure that one out," said Beamer. "The hard part's not the commands but how to say them. A couple days ago Dad found a website on American dialects, so Mom's gettin' the hang of it. The phone's over there ... uh ... Ghoulie. Is it really *Ghoulie*?"

"No," he said shrugging, "but Ghoulie's what everyone calls me." He threw down his leather-tooled backpack and picked up the receiver. He couldn't remember when somebody had first called him that, but it had stuck.

"Do you want me to call you something else?"

"No, that's okay. I don't particularly like my real name either. It's Garfunkel—Garfunkel Ives to be more exact." The name had come from some musician back in the sixties and seventies, so his parents had told him. But what kind of nickname could you make out of Garfunkel? Garf? Funkel?

The microwave oven beeped. As Beamer started toward it, Michael burst through the door and crowded in front of him to pull out a steaming bag of popcorn.

"Keep your pinkies out of my bag," Michael said, stuffing

his face full of white kernels.

"Share, Michael!" called their mother from another room.

While Beamer and Michael continued their daily after-school squabble, a girl with blonde hair bounded through the door. "Mom!" she yelled. "Everybody's thirsty upstairs, with all the heat and stuff." *Has to be the sister.*

"Okay," Mrs. Mac called in again. "There are extra sodas and lots of water bottles in the refrigerator on the back porch."

"Thanks!" the girl shouted cheerfully as she dashed out to the back porch.

Ghoulie heard his nanny's voice on the phone and clapped his hand over an ear, trying to screen out the noise. "No, I'm okay!" he shouted into the phone. "No, you don't need to call Dad ..." *Why does she always have to panic?*

Carrying a frosty six-pack of soft drinks, the girl danced back into the kitchen, twirled around like a ballet dancer, and glided through the hallway door.

"Hey, what's with her?" Beamer asked Michael.

"D'ya remember the guy who barged into her room by mistake?"

"Yeah, the scientist guy."

"Well, turns out he's gorgeous," Michael finished, stretching out the word to mock his sister's mushy description. He sucked up a handful of popcorn like a vacuum and charged out of the kitchen.

"Really, I can just—" stammered Ghoulie, his attention drawn back to the frantic woman on the phone. "Okay, okay, I'll keep an eye out for him." He sighed and hung up, then turned to find himself alone in the kitchen. He wandered onto the back porch and looked out at the backyard. One thing his family's high-end condominium didn't have was a backyard. Hearing something creaking in the wind, he walked out the door.

The screen door slammed behind him and he heard something creak again, this time directly above him. He looked up. "A tree house!" he blurted out in envy.

"You don't want to go up there!" Scilla's voice called from the next yard. "I told you. It's haunted."

Ghoulie glanced from her back up at the tree house. "The tree house? I thought you meant the house!"

"The house may be too, for all I know. But the tree house is a definite," Scilla said as she swung up onto a branch.

"Whoever heard of a haunted tree house?" asked Ghoulie as he crab-walked up the slanted trunk. He figured he had maybe ten minutes before his dad got there, but he could at least get a closer look.

"Get real, Scilla!" groaned a voice below him. Ghoulie turned to see Beamer at the foot of the tree, starting to crab-walk up toward them.

Ghoulie turned back to Scilla. "Even if there were a ghost," he added with a smirk, "it couldn't be much of a ghost if it lives in a tree house."

"It was enough of a ghost to scare the heck out of Jared!"

It was like Scilla had exploded a cherry bomb. "D'ya mean Jared's been here?" Beamer yelped, bumping his head on a branch above him and nearly falling out of the tree.

"Priscilla! Priscilla!" an elderly woman's voice called, "Did you forget that you're grounded today?" It was Scilla's grandmother, calling from the second-story window at the near end of her house. "You come home right now and get busy on that homework, or you'll be grounded for a month!"

"Oops, I gotta go," Scilla said with a fearful grimace, already scooting along the tree branch that crossed over into her yard.

"Scillaaaa! You can't go now!" Beamer yelled after her, irritated at being unable to hear the rest of the story.

"Sorry!" she called back as she dropped from the tree, "I'll see y'all tomorrow."

Ghoulie gave Beamer a frustrated look. Their eyes locked meaningfully. Gulping in unison, they looked wide-eyed up at the tree house.

10

Reluctant Ghostbusters

The day after the chase through the park, Beamer gave Jared double the amount due, plus a nauseating truckload of "Sorrys." Just to make sure Jared didn't give him a knuckle sandwich for change, Beamer paid him off before assembly in front of the teacher seats.

Of course, the real question was how this underage "C-movie" schmuck could keep getting away with stomping on everyone. All the kids were sure he was skimming off milk money for himself. By all rights, he should have been hauled into the principal's office a hundred times since school started.

A few days later, the answer crashed down on Beamer like a load of bricks. He was leaving the library with a book on Greek myths for his book report (the choice was either Greek heroes or guppy fishing in Saskatchewan), when he saw Jared down the corridor. He was standing beside a woman—his mother, from the looks of it—who was talking with the principal. For one brief shining moment, Beamer's hopes leaped. *Maybe this is it. Justice has finally caught up with him.*

One problem: the two grown-ups looked far too cheerful. Then, with a jolt that shook Beamer down to his size-eight Nikes, he realized the bitter truth: Jared's mom and the principal were friends—buddies!

*   *   *   *   *

That afternoon Beamer watched the last half of *E. T.* He didn't feel like cartoons, and it wasn't his day for video games. He turned the TV off after Elliot and E.T. rode across the moon and set up that "phone home" contraption in the forest.

Beamer wandered into the backyard, kicking along a rock as he walked. *"Home" for me is still Shadow Beach Lane in California, not Murphy Street in some nowhere called Middleton.*

One last kick sent the rock tumbling into the garage. Everything inside the garage was connected to everything else by spiderwebs and coated with dust an inch thick. Everything, that is, except for his mom.

"Hi, Beamer," she said, turning to him. "Look what I found." She pointed to several rows of barrels, then to a rust-plated, mechanical nightmare that looked like it was for embalming mummies.

"What is it?" he asked.

"A molasses cooker," she replied. "The barrels are full of the stuff, though it's mostly turned to sugar now. Somebody a long time ago had a little home business going here."

"What do you do with it?" Beamer asked, glancing around disapprovingly.

"It's like syrup. Nowadays they sell it at fairs and have

contests. If I can get this contraption working," she added, turning a knob on the cooker, "I think I might try and heat what's in those barrels back into molasses and see what happens."

Beamer shrugged and turned away with a heavy sigh. His mom—a pediatrician, healer of children, and handyman extraordinaire—reduced to playing with antique pancake syrup! Would this move to Murphy Street leave her no shred of dignity?

He heard a noise at the driveway gate.

"Hey, Beamer," said Ghoulie, giving him a wave. "Could I have a look at your tree house?"

"You sure y'all want to do that?" yelled Scilla from her upstairs window. "Remember what happened to Jared."

"That's the point," Ghoulie shouted back to her. "Anything that's bad for Jared has got to be good for us."

Beamer opened the gate and let Ghoulie in. "So what happened in the tree house that caused him to go nuts?" he yelled up toward Scilla's window. But the window was now empty.

Ghoulie crab-walked up the tree, eyeing the tree house with anticipation. "Were there any electronic pulses, atmospheric distortions, or ectoplasmic manifestations when Jared went up there?"

Scilla, now standing on the ground directly below them, stared at him like he had antennae and green skin. "Uhh ... my grandma doesn't let me see very many movies."

"Scillaaaa!" Beamer yelled impatiently. "Tell us what happened!"

She leaped and swung herself up on the branch. "Jared rides his bike down Parkview Court up there every Saturday on his way home from the movies. He'd heard about the tree house being haunted and came over to check it out—him and his Skullcross Gang."

"Skullcross?!" Beamer exclaimed.

"Yeah, that's what they call themselves," Ghoulie added. "They've got this insignia that looks like a pirate's flag except it's got crossed money in front of a skull instead of crossed bones."

"Money ... it figures," Beamer grunted. "Go on," he said to Scilla.

"Well, he bashed through the door into the tree ship," she continued. "I heard weird clicking sounds and a roaring like the wind and it got louder and louder. The next thing I knew, he came outta there like he was on fire and scrambled down the tree so fast he was practically fallin'. Of course, he told everybody he fought off the ghost and wrecked the place, but I knew things weren't exactly like he'd said."

"Jared ... scared out of a tree house," Ghoulie mumbled in awe.

Beamer started climbing up toward the tree house. "You guys coming or not?" he threw back over his shoulder.

Scilla gave Ghoulie a look, took a deep breath, and started after Beamer.

Beamer made his way up quickly through the maze of branches. Scilla and Ghoulie were on his tail as if they were walking through a minefield. But when the last spread of leaves cleared before Beamer, he slowed. There it was—even bigger than he had thought—about as long as a good-sized camper and half as wide across.

Before long they could see the tree house's—that is, ship's—long fuselage suspended between the two trunks of the tree. "Man, this is awesome!" Beamer exclaimed as they passed in front of an outrigger engine.

"Yeah ... well the birds think so too," Ghoulie wise-cracked as he peered into it. "There's a nest inside. So much for warp speed."

Soon they stepped down to a large branch and gazed across a short wooden ramp. It was more like a rope bridge, and it swung in the wind. On the other side was the tree ship door.

"Well, here goes," Beamer said with a gulp. Hesitantly he stepped onto the ramp. A sudden gust of wind made the bridge sway like a boat in a rough sea.

He backed into them against the tree, holding tight, afraid to move. "Uh ... ladies first," he stammered. "Go ahead, Scilla."

"Forget it," Scilla gulped. "We've been liberated. We don't hafta go first anymore. Besides, it's *your* tree!" she added sassily.

"Okay ... okay," Beamer groaned. The ramp was swinging wildly in the wind now while the door at the other end, already half-wrenched off its hinges, was banging mercilessly against the tree ship wall.

All sorts of pictures raced through his mind as he inched his way across the bridge. Scenes from every thriller he'd ever seen (or thought of seeing) pummeled his imagination. There were hairy, slavering beasts with big lips; oozing ectoplasmic blobs who belched when they sucked you up; cyborgs with red eyeballs, metal jeans and anti-gravity loafers; mutant slugs that left trails of electromagnetic ooze ... Of course, his mom and dad never let him see the really gory movies, but, when it came to mean and ugly, he'd imagined it.

He was about to go into "C-movie" overload when a major gust blew him crashing to the floor. While he lay there, reeling with dizziness, other noises—buzzing and clicking—began to grow louder.

"Holy tamole! What's goin' on?!" Scilla exclaimed as she and Ghoulie suddenly appeared, crouching beside him.

"There wasn't any windstorm in the online weather report," Ghoulie piped up.

"I don't know," Beamer said weakly. "Maybe this tree has its own weather pattern."

"Or maybe this place *really is* haunted," Ghoulie suggested, just as feebly.

A cricket, looking not the least bit scared, hopped between Beamer's feet, then through the door opening, and disappeared. As if on cue, the wind and insect noises seemed to lessen. Beamer looked into the dark interior of the tree ship and took another deep breath. He might be one step away from being either totally dematerialized or severely slimed.

With a "Here goes," he shoved what was left of the door aside and vaulted inside. Immediately an electronic crackle sent him whirling around.

11
Crash Landing

"Log on," an electronic voice beeped. "Please log on—name and Starrr-Fiiightrrr co-o-o-o-ode." Then it sputtered and stopped like a toy winding down.

"Ohhh boy," Beamer muttered as he moved away from the wall. It took a moment for his eyes to adjust. What light there was seeped in through the cracks in the walls.

"Keep an eye out for anything slimy," Ghoulie whispered loudly through the door.

"Or what's left of somebody's guts," Scilla added.

The ship creaked in the wind, though the other noises seemed to be dying now. He listened carefully for heavy breathing, something burbling or groaning or roaring or sizzling.

Then a surge of light blinded him.

"Hey!!" he cried, spinning around.

"A window!" Ghoulie said triumphantly, looking

through a large opening.

There were two such windows on each side of the ship, which opened by sliding away a piece of plywood. Now revealed were the remains of broken tables holding bashed-in plywood instrument panels.

"I don't see anything that looks remotely slimy," Scilla said after an express tour.

"Not even scary," Beamer added. "Just messy." Limbs, leaves, pieces of wood, and junk were all over the place. "You don't suppose Jared's afraid of dirt?"

"The way he rubs people's faces in it, not likely," Ghoulie said as he crossed to open another window.

"Lot's of wildlife here, though," Scilla said, noting several crickets hopping about. "Especially tree crickets."

"Yeah, I know," Beamer responded. "Don't smush 'em. My mom likes 'em."

"Grandma says they're good luck," Scilla continued, peering at a cricket perched at eye level in the window opening. "Somethin' about givin' peace to your home."

"Well, from the looks of things," said Beamer, "there's been no peace around here for quite a while." He wiped his hand across a table, sending several decades' worth of collected leaves, twigs, dirt, and dead bugs sliding to the floor.

Ghoulie found the device responsible for that electronic password message. It was a primitive computer hooked up to a cassette recorder. "A little dated, but it works ... uh, did work," he said, examining the setup.

"Look at this stuff," Beamer exclaimed as his eyes scanned the array of dials, handles, and switches set up on the tables. "Strictly Stone Age!"

The ceiling was curved high enough for adults to stand only in the middle. Beamer wandered toward the nose of the tree ship. Reaching over the battered control panel, he slid back another plywood window. Light flooded into the cockpit. He could see the tree and the blue sky beyond the tree ship's stubby nose.

Beamer ran his hands slowly along what was left of an instrument panel. "Man, it must have been some crash," he said to himself.

"What did you say?" Ghoulie asked, turning toward him.

"This ship ... It had a bad landing."

His hands began moving rapidly over the controls, pushing buttons, pulling down levers.

Suddenly beeps, pings, and other audio signals began to be heard all over the ship.

"Reverse thrusters!" Beamer yelled. The hum of engines filled the tree ship. Lighted dials, flashing panels, graphic displays were everywhere, reflecting off the ceiling, the kids' faces.... "Activate the anti-gravity array ... now!" Beamer cried again.

Ghoulie and Scilla looked at him like he'd lost a few screws. "Who does he think he is, Captain Kirk?" Ghoulie whispered to Scilla.

Suddenly the ship lurched, throwing them to the floor. They pulled themselves back up and wondered if they had suffered brain damage. For there was Beamer, (though not the Beamer they knew) standing before them in a red, yellow, and blue uniform with brass buttons.

"Officer Ives!" he barked. "Snap to it! We are on a collision course!"

Ghoulie looked out the window and, sure enough, there was a blue and white globe below them, growing steadily bigger before their eyes. What was going on? Were they in some kind of daydream?

Then, like the last pieces in a puzzle, Ghoulie and Scilla suddenly popped into full-uniform and snapped into the story. Their hands flashed across instrument panels as if they'd been born to it.

"'Aye, Captain!" Ghoulie shouted. "Thrusters are in full reverse, but energy levels are down seventy percent. Lieutenant Bruzelski!" he called, turning to Scilla. "The anti-gravity array!"

"Uh, right," she said, as an instrument panel spit out a plume of smoke. "Sorry, Commander," she said weakly, "the anti-gravity array is ... a goner."

"Try the gluon particle zapper!" Beamer ordered, "Or was that the stickyon matter gummerupper? Whatever ... do it!"

Ghoulie read the data on his holographic computer display, then looked up through the cockpit window. Shandar Three, or Earth, or Terra, or whatever it was called, depending upon which native tribe you asked, was coming up fast.

"We're entering the atmosphere!" Ghoulie announced.

"She's starting to buck!" Scilla warned. Immediately her body began jerking about as if she were riding a roller coaster.

"Bruzelski!" Beamer shouted. "See if you can ice down the heat shield. At the rate we're dropping, things are going to get french fried around here real soon."

"'Aye, Captain!" She ran to an instrument panel in the back wall and ripped off the facing. Sparks flickered and flared like the Fourth of July.

Beamer jammed a lever hard to the right, then looked up to the window again. The ship's nose glowed a pale red. "We're cooking!"

Ghoulie and Scilla saw sparks zipping past the side windows. They could hear a whine growing louder. Ghoulie wiped sweat from his brow with one hand while the other danced across the dials. "I think I'm getting something, Captain. She's pulling up ... or over ... or something!"

"Got to have more!" Beamer shouted. "Bruzelski, what's happening back there?"

"They're frozen, sir ... the controls," she grunted as she leaned on a lever with all of her seventy-five pounds. "Wait! It's moving!"

But the ship was already too low. It was coming down like a meteor in a blaze of fire. The crystal-Albumidium magnetronic outer coating had already melted. The sillidium shell went next, followed by the megabidium, then the jillibidium, and all the other idium layers.

"Captain!" Ghoulie shouted. "We're being peeled like an onion. Another ten seconds and we'll be fireworks!"

Then Beamer saw it — something rising from the edge of a small primitive city, reaching toward them. A faint siren sounded in the background. Tendrils wrapped around the ship like a squid about to have lunch and pulled her down.

"What's happening?" cried Scilla.

"We're caught in some kind of ... biological nightmare — hard, crusty limbs, draped with green stuff, coming out of the ground reaching into the sky.... Release the orthomoponic plantipus delimiter," Ghoulie cried.

"The what?" Scilla asked.

"The weed killer!" Ghoulie yelled. But once again it was too late.

There was a PHUD, a CRUNCH, and a rustle-rustle. The ship was stuck — in something the crew would later learn was called a "tree." All that was left of her eight-layer hull was the frame, swaying in the branches.

"Beamer!" his mother's voice called from the back door. Beamer, Ghoulie, and Scilla looked at each other in bewilderment. They were their old selves again—shorts, jeans, T-shirts, ponytail, and all. The instrument panels were again broken plywood with painted dials and broom handle levers.

That night, after everyone else had fallen asleep, Beamer crawled out his window and sat on his roof staring at the tree ship. He couldn't see much of it in the light of a half moon, but he had a flashlight.

What was going on? He spotlighted first the ramp, then the door. It hadn't been your usual "let's pretend" experience—it had been more like a parallel universe or something ... where almost everything is the same but some things are different.

His mom had said it was just his super-charged imagination. Maybe, but he hadn't had anything so totally off-the-wall, suck-up-your-brain real in a long time. It was like being a character in your own video game—virtual reality way beyond virtual.

He panned his flashlight across the tree ship's surface like a searchlight. *Maybe it is haunted after all.*

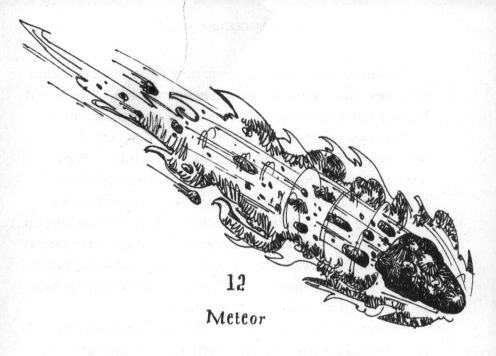

12

Meteor

Weeks passed. Squirt guns and water slides were replaced by footballs and crisp, multicolored leaves piled high for diving into. Beamer spent countless hours in the tree ship with his new friends.

And his family found a good church to attend, much to the relief of Beamer's parents, who insisted they all attend not only Sunday morning service, but Sunday evening, as well. When the kids protested, Dr. Mac reminded them that this church was their new "family" now, and it was time to get to know their relatives.

Secretly, though, Beamer was happy to settle into the well-worn cushions twice each weekend. He missed his old church and all his church friends. Plus, this church had something new to offer: the scent of warming casseroles and baking desserts wafting from the church basement promising a scrumptious potluck dinner after services.

Besides church, weekends were now filled with Boy Scout activities. That's how, one Saturday afternoon, Beamer found himself standing before a big rock in the park museum.

The boys' rating system for the exhibits had ranged from empty stares to snickering. The biggest hit had been a statue—okay, sculpture—made out of clothespins and hubcaps. It hadn't been a good day for the arts in America.

But here they were in front of this big rock. The writing on the plaque said the rock was a meteor. To an old space trader like Beamer, that was news in itself. It didn't look like much, though—no star-shaped crystal, pulsing with energy. It was just a shiny, dark rock with a chip missing.

No wonder I'm still in Middleton, thought Beamer, as he remembered his wish that first night in town. *Anyone who believes some gnarly old rock can grant wishes needs to have his head examined. Still, it is from another world.*

The plaque read: "Found July 20, 1919, at a site 877 yards west of its present location."

West? Beamer thought about it: *Let's see, west is that-away—over toward Murphy Street.* He tried to remember how long a yard was. One thing was for sure: he was going to work harder on the weights and measurement tables. *Okay, let's see ... there are a hundred yards in a football playing field. That would make it just under nine football fields to where the meteor landed, which would put it—*

All at once the image of the split tree trunk burst into his imagination. His eyes grew wide. *You don't suppose ... What if this meteor crashed into* my *tree?*

Twenty minutes later, scout compass in hand, Beamer was stepping off huge steps due west from the museum. "Forty-seven, forty-eight, forty-nine—"

He glanced up. *Yep, so far, so good.* The way led right up to the brick wall. He'd just walk it off to there, then pick it up again when he went around to the other side of the wall—as long as it wasn't Ms. Parker's yard, that is.

With his eyeball planted on his compass, Beamer didn't notice what was going on around him. So, when he looked up again, he was totally unprepared to see a football on a trajectory straight for his nose.

All Beamer could do was open his mouth. For that matter, nothing else would move. He watched the perfect spiral plummeting toward him like a dark falling star. He could see the little puckered seams and the threads spinning slowly around. One microsecond before he was to lose his face, a pair of hands erupted into the picture and caught the ball. Then the body attached to those hands slammed into Beamer like a Mac truck.

* * * * *

The next thing Beamer knew, he was laid out on his bed with three Moms hovering above him. Something was definitely unscrewed in his brain. He saw her mouth (or mouths) moving, but all he could hear was a roaring sound, like from a waterfall.

She stroked Beamer's hair fondly. "Oom-aa-faaa-blll-yrsssss-braww-ooo-omm" is what he heard her say. Later he learned that one of the football players, who also happened to be the paperboy, had brought him home. Her lips were moving again: "Oooollll-beee-aaaallll-riiii-ohhh-yrrrr-goiing-taaave-a-ud-siize-knot-on-heedd," he heard.

The doorbell rang. "I'll be right back," she said and hurried out of the room.

As her footsteps tripped lightly down the staircase, he heard a noise above the ceiling—something crashing. The scientists weren't working in the attic today, so there shouldn't have been anyone up there to break something. He sat up, and then grabbed his head with a heavy groan. Feeling a little better, he shook his head and wobbled through his door and into the hallway. At that moment a kitten slipped from behind the attic door, which somebody had apparently left ajar.

"Lacy!" Beamer yelled after her. "You're not supposed to be up there!"

It was Erin's cat—the result of a deal she hadn't been able to refuse when her mom had sent her to the nearby mini-market last week. *If those scientist guys find out a cat's been up around their equipment, they'll be* ... Beamer opened the attic door and, holding the rail firmly, slowly stumbled up the steps. He wasn't supposed to go into the attic, but he thought he might be able to fix what the cat had done. At least, that was going to be his excuse if he was caught. What he really wanted, of course, was to see what was going on with the now famous "MacIntyre web."

The attic was bright this time of day, with beams from the low-hanging sun blasting through the large back windows. Beamer was more concerned, though, about the dark shadows—about whether anything with eight legs and man-eating mandibles was hiding in them. After a careful scan with his super peepers, he relaxed. Anyway, if the entomologists hadn't seen the creature in all the weeks they'd been up here, he figured he was pretty safe.

At the moment, though, with all the scientific equipment planted around it, the web looked more like a web Darth Vader built. Toss out the web and combine the windows into a view screen, and the attic might look like the bridge of a starship. The web was awesome. Glowing golden-yellow in the evening light, it cast a huge shadow across one whole side of the attic, including Beamer's face. It made him feel very uneasy, and he kept wiping his face, trying to rub off the web that wasn't really there.

The mystery of the web was growing almost every day. Its silk threads were thicker than those in normal webs, and they were enormously strong. The big question, of course, was *What* or *Who* built it? One entomologist thought some mad scientist had created it for a weird experiment. All the rest were sticking to the mutant-spider theory. Their research had led them to agree on only one thing—that the web had been built a long time ago—maybe eighty or ninety years ago. That made the chances of either the mad scientist or the mutant still being alive pretty remote ... although the word *mutant* suggested all sorts of possibilities. Beamer also wondered why nobody had reported the web until now. Hadn't anybody used the attic before Beamer's family moved in?

New mysteries were always popping up too. Beamer had heard a scientist—the one his sister had a crush on—say that he'd detected a faint electro ... something ... field around the web. *Whoever heard of an electric cobweb?*

The shadow of the web on Beamer's face made him anxious to leave. But before he left, he scanned the room for any sign of wreckage from the cat. He sighed in relief when he saw that the only thing broken was a soda bottle. He picked up as many pieces as he could and deposited them up next to the wall.

Parker's Castle was framed through one of the front windows. He couldn't see anyone in the tower, but he knew she was there. He'd seen her there often enough, usually after dark when the lights were on and he could see her shadow silhouetted in the window.

He looked the other direction—out the back window. There was the tree ship. He walked over to the window, opened it, and stepped out onto the roof. He then scooted down the shingles, swung onto a large tree branch, and made his way to the tree ship.

It was very quiet at the moment—hardly a breeze—with only a few insect noises. As Beamer looked at the ship, he could see how much progress they'd already made in fixing it up. Scilla had been replacing the broken chairs with her grandma's garage-sale rejects.

Beamer, meanwhile, had been working on the problem of, well, beaming. Let's face it, as things stood now, getting into the tree ship was a major chore. Molecular dematerialization was a little beyond him at this point, but he had some ideas.

One glance at Beamer trying to stretch an extension cord to the tree had already persuaded Dr. Mac to string heavy-duty electrical conduit from the attic to the tree ship. She even went so far as to suspend a huge fishing net beneath the tree to catch anyone who might miss a step.

The observation screen was Ghoulie's project. "On-screen" wasn't going to mean quite what it did on *Star Trek*, but it wasn't going to be half bad for seventh-grade engineering. Anyway, it would become real enough when their brains warped into full-blown Star-Fighter mode. Yep, that's what the ship told them they were—Star-Fighters.

"Hey!"

Beamer turned to see Scilla's face upside down in a window. No sooner had they started working on their respective fix-up operations than they heard another voice: "Hello up there," Ghoulie called.

Ghoulie had brought one of his dad's old video cameras

to hang beneath the ship, and, considering that Ghoulie's dad always snatched up the latest high-tech upgrades, "old" meant last July's model. Ditto for the wide-angle, high-res, glue-ya-to-the-tube video screen.

While the ship was looking better, they hadn't yet figured out what was going on with their blow-em-outta-the-sky adventures. It only happened once in awhile, and they could never predict when. Beamer thought they came more often after he'd had a bad day at school with Jared.

"He's got to have a weak spot, you know," said Beamer, out of the blue.

"Who?" asked Ghoulie.

"Who do you think? Jared, of course! He must have an Achilles' heel! We've just got to find it."

"Kill what?" asked a confused Scilla.

"Not kill," said Ghoulie, rolling his eyes. "A-kill-eez—the Greek hero."

"He was invincible," explained Beamer, "except for one weak spot—his heel. That's how they got him—shot him in the heel."

Suddenly a rumble like a train approaching shook the tree, rattling the tree ship like a box of toys, throwing each of them to the floor.

13

The Return of the Star-Fighters

When they opened their eyes, the ship was on fire! Or was it? Beamer looked out the view port. Filling the screen was the face of a planet—a planet on fire! A moon-sized, crater-pitted asteroid had just collided with the planet, shattering its hard outer shell—causing the fiery molten core to erupt into space like splattering catsup.

Their ship, meanwhile, was whirling through space like a corkscrew roller coaster.

"Captain MacIntyre! Gravitational controls!" a voice commanded.

The part of the Captain that was still Beamer turned to see Scilla looking very grown-up and very much in command.

"We've got gravity from the planet and the asteroid hitting us at the same time!" Ghoulie shouted from a smoking, sparking control panel. "Engines and shields are off-line, Admiral Bruzelski!"

Admiral? How did she get to be "Admiral"? part of Beamer's mind asked.

Globs of red molten lava were being flung their way like massive paint balls. "We are about to be spattered by some very hot spaghetti!" yelled Beamer. "... with meatballs!" he then added, seeing monstrous, jagged fragments from both the planet and the asteroid tumbling toward them like a sidewise avalanche.

"Get those engines fired up now, Captain!" cried the Admiral. "Commander Ives, direct reverse tractor beam at those lava flares!"

Beamer rushed toward the trap door, dived through the floor, and started ripping out circuit boards.

Suddenly the ship rocked violently, like they'd been smacked with a giant flyswatter. "Hull's still intact!" Ghoulie assured them. "But we won't be able to handle many more impacts like that."

Beamer jammed a new electronic panel into a slot and the ship suddenly surged into darkness. He fell backward into another panel which sparked and sizzled like he was sausage in a frying pan. "Yeow!" he yelped as he leaped back to the main deck.

"Talk about the nick of time!" yelled Scilla. "Good job, MacIntyre. Ives, we're jumping blind! Put us back into normal space before we jump into the middle of a sun!"

The engines cut off and they were again in normal space. Then Beamer noticed that fire still filled one of the view screens. "Hey! Didn't we go anywhere?"

"What's the matter with navigation?" asked the Admiral.

"We've moved," said Ghoulie. "We did — about three hundred million kilometers!"

"Then where are we, and why do I feel like I'm being bar-bequed?" demanded Scilla, wiping sweat from her face.

Beamer decreased magnification on the view port. Something that looked like a humongous, thick, fiery rope stretched across the sky. At either end of the rope were two stars — one large and red, the other smaller and white.

"Ach! The noise!" cried Beamer, holding his ears.

"It's a massive energy stream!" Ghoulie shouted. "The suns in this binary system are so close together they're stealing energy from each other."

The sound of static on their sensors was deafening. Beamer ran to an instrument panel and flipped the speakers off. He glanced over at the dark view port on the other side of the ship. "There goes the planet!" he yelled, seeing the tiny, distant flare of the exploding planet.

A much brighter flash suddenly streaked past them, then another. The ship quaked each time, like they had suddenly dropped a few floors in an elevator. Beamer readjusted the view port displaying the two suns and then instinctively ducked as a blinding fireball skimmed across the screen. "Hey, haven't you guys ever heard of water balloons?" he yelled at the two suns, which seemed to be hurling energy plumes at each other.

"Get us out of here, Commander! Now!" ordered Scilla.

Again the screens streaked into darkness. A few moments later the ship once more emerged into normal space. Or was it? The black velvet sky ahead of the ship was ablaze with stars — millions of them — rolled into a bright, raggedy ball.

"We're right next door to a globular star cluster," announced Ghoulie. They suddenly felt the ship shudder. "Now what?" groaned Ghoulie as he checked his sensors. "Shock waves, lots of them on all sides!"

Another glance at the view ports made their situation clear. They were in the middle of a fleet of space ships.

"It's a whole armada!" Ghoulie gasped. Checking his sensor screens again, he continued, "They're using pre-hyperspace technology — traveling at sub-light speeds. We can easily outrun them."

"I'm just glad they don't seem to be trigger happy. Hail them!" ordered Scilla.

"I am," answered Ghoulie. "All I'm getting is a recording and — surprise, surprise — they don't speak our language."

One corner of Ghoulie's mind made a note to paint a universal translator into the ship before their next trip.

"See if you can hack into their computer systems," ordered Scilla.

Moments later the view screen displayed a series of pictures like you'd see from surveillance cameras. Their gasp nearly sucked the air out of the ship. Rows and rows of what looked like transparent cigars, set on end, lined ten decks of a very large ship.

"Magnify!" ordered Scilla.

Beamer adjusted the view screens. Encased within those fat cylinders were bodies.

"It's a ghost ship!" exclaimed Beamer.

"Yeah, as in bug ghosts," gulped Ghoulie.

The bodies, which seemed to be swimming in a cloudy yellowish mist, had large insect eyes, armored torsos and — exactly how many they couldn't see — definitely more than two legs.

"Oops," corrected Ghoulie. "Guess what? They're alive."

"D'ya mean they're asleep?" stammered Beamer.

"Yep, they're all nighty-night in suspended animation," added Ghoulie.

"So that's why they're not shooting at us," said Scilla.

"I've calculated their origin," said Ghoulie as his hands skipped over the instruments. "They're from the exploding planet. Left several months ago, I'd guess."

"Refugees, eh. Heading where?" asked Scilla.

"Toward the globular cluster," answered Ghoulie. "At their present speed it'll take them years to get there. We'll probably be ghosts before they find a suitable planet."

"Somebody's in for a major alien invasion if they choose one with indigenous, intelligent life forms," muttered Scilla.

"At least they won't be looking for an earth-type planet," said Ghoulie. "The yellowish mist in those canisters isn't oxygen/nitrogen."

"Priscilla! Priscilla!" a woman's voice called. "Are you all right, honey?"

Scilla blinked and winced, once again a girl in jeans and ponytail. "I'm fine, Grandma," she said, leaning out the window. "What's the matter?"

"Didn't you feel the quake?" Grandma held a hand over her chest, breathing heavily. "It nearly shook my china to the floor. Come on down, now. I don't want you up a tree if there's an aftershock."

"Okay, I'll be right down," Scilla called to her.

"Earthquakes? Here?" Beamer asked.

Ghoulie laughed. "I thought you wanted reminders of home."

"Yeah, I had everything in California," Beamer said wistfully. "Friends, sports, secret bases all over the place, and no—read my lips—no Jared. Here, I'm an alien, just like those bug-faced guys in the fleet are gonna be."

"I've been here all my life and I'm still an alien," shrugged Ghoulie. He turned to Scilla and said, "You're just lucky you're a girl."

"Hey, it isn't so easy being a girl either, especially if you hate skirts and hair straighteners," she retorted. "You don't have to have muscles to be a bully, you know. Girls have other ways to bully."

"I'm sorry, I didn't realize," Ghoulie said with a sheepish look.

"So I guess we're all aliens, huh," shrugged Beamer.

"With our very own hostile indigenous life forms," Ghoulie grumbled.

"What's in-didge-nous?" Scilla asked, her head popping back into sight.

Beamer and Ghoulie gave each other a knowing look, then looked back at Scilla and said, at the same time, "Jared!"

*   *   *   *   *

Defeating their hostile indigenous life form wouldn't be easy. In fact, Beamer figured that finding Jared's Achilles' heel was going to be something on the order of finding a snowflake in the Sahara. Here was a pimple-faced muscle-machine who had manipulating adults down to a science, and who also happened to be the principal's pet. The prospects didn't look good.

Then, out of nowhere, the Star-Fighters got a break.

14

Achilles' Heel

It didn't seem like much of a break at first. Jared and the other eighth graders were doing math problems at a blackboard when the teacher stepped out to answer a call. Jared, meanwhile, turned the place into a casino, and by the time the teacher got back, he had fleeced a schmuck who didn't know how to play 3-D tic-tac-toe and had a week's worth of the kid's milk money.

It didn't figure to be a major setback for Jared—not with *his* connections. Everybody expected the principal to just waggle a friendly finger, make him give back the money, and send her regards to his mother. In fact, that's what actually happened.

The break came from the fact that Jared had to wait

for the principal. All he had with him was his notebook. So, he sat alone in a corner and waited ... and waited ...

He eventually started fidgeting. One particular fidget allowed him to see a pencil under the bench. He picked it up and, after a quick look around to make sure nobody was watching, started to doodle.

*   *   *   *   *

Jared left the principal's office just in time for the final bell. Kids were scurrying up and down the hallway like mice in a cheese factory.

Beamer and Ghoulie entered the hall in time to see a worried-looking Jared dash into the restroom. *What was this? Jared without the smirk? Jared ... afraid?*

Barely half a minute later, Jared came out of the restroom, still looking worried and glancing around. *Something is missing. He'd had something when he went into the bathroom that he didn't have now. What was it?* Then it struck Beamer. *He'd ditched his notebook. Why?*

Beamer and Ghoulie quickly pretended to be in a heated discussion. "Come on, Ghoulie," Beamer insisted, "*Nestle* makes the best chocolate."

"Hey, forget it," Ghoulie shot back. "*Hershey* ... man ... that's the ticket." (Well, what would you expect from seventh graders, the stock-market report?)

Jared quickly assumed his cool, macho look and swaggered off down the hall.

"Let's check it out!" Beamer said, and streaked into the bathroom like it was a candy store.

"What do you suppose he was up to?" Ghoulie asked as he peered into the corners of the starkly institutional bathroom. Then he dug into a trash can.

"I don't know," Beamer said, searching through another

can, "but he was in a big hurry to get rid of that notebook. I got a good feeling about it." Beamer pulled several crumpled sheets of paper from the trash can.

"Find anything?" Ghoulie asked, walking over to him.

"Just a bunch of drawings—butterflies, birds, flowers, trees, and stuff."

"Hey, they're not bad," Ghoulie said. "Not bad at all. Who do you suppose drew them?"

"How should I know?" Beamer responded, reaching deeper into the trash can. He pulled out a notebook. "Here's some more," he said as he leafed through half-torn-out pages.

Ghoulie took the notebook and turned it over. "Cowabunga!" he said in a hushed voice, staring at the back cover.

"Skullcross!" Beamer exclaimed, looking at a picture of a skull and crisscrossing dollar signs drawn in masterful strokes. "These are Jared's?" he gasped.

"We got him!" Ghoulie said, his eyes as bright as searchlights. He stuffed the drawings into the notebook and bolted out the door.

"Drawings? He wanted to hide drawings?" Beamer asked in confusion as he hurried up behind Ghoulie. "Why?"

"This is Jared we're dealing with," Ghoulie said, cruising down the hallway wearing a first-class grin. "Bullies don't draw cute little pictures."

"But they're good!" Beamer said with a troubled look.

"Maybe!" Ghoulie said through clenched teeth. "But to Jared they're an Achilles' heel."

"Ghoulie, are you sure ...?" Beamer murmured.

"Sure about what?" he returned as he shot out the rear entrance. He stopped to scan the playground. "Come on," Ghoulie said as he ran out across the playground.

"Hey, y'all!" called Scilla, who was running after them.

"Whatch y'all up to?"

"Look at this!" Ghoulie said, thrusting a crumpled paper into her hands.

"A drawing," she said with a shrug. "So?"

"It's Jared's," Ghoulie announced, like he'd just discovered the ruins of Atlantis. He accelerated down the block toward the boulevard.

When they finally stopped for the light, Scilla grabbed Beamer's arm. "What are y'all goin' to do?" she asked, gasping for air. Across the street the park spread out before them like a vast wilderness.

"Look, he's scared of people finding out he draws these things," Ghoulie explained impatiently. "That's his Achilles' heel! All we have to do is threaten to show these all over the school and he'll stop buggin' us."

"Ghoulie . . . ," Beamer started to say as the light changed. Ghoulie ran across the street with Beamer and Scilla in his wake and plunged into the thick woods.

The forest path was like a tall corridor walled with trees. Racing around a curve they saw Jared far ahead.

"There he is!" Ghoulie exclaimed. "This is perfect! We can do it now!"

"Ghoulie, shouldn't we think this over?" Beamer stammered, half out of breath.

"What's to think over? He's alone now, can't you see? Who knows when we'll have another chance like this. Scilla can hide out in the bushes with most of the drawings while we show Jared a few samples to let him know we have the goods."

"Ghoulie! No!" Beamer cried, grabbing Ghoulie's arm and whirling him around.

"What's the matter with you?" Ghoulie asked, looking at Beamer like his brain had come unscrewed.

"This isn't right!"

"Are you crazy?" Ghoulie yelled, about to come unscrewed himself. "We've got what we've been looking for. We've found his Achilles' heel!"

"No we haven't!" Beamer said, breathing hard. "We said an Achilles' heel was a weak spot. This isn't a weakness," he said, gesturing to the notebook. "It's a . . . a . . ."

"Come on!" Ghoulie said, turning away from him. "He'll get away." Suddenly Beamer grabbed the notebook and dashed into the forest.

"Beamer!" Ghoulie shrieked as he rushed after him.

In the distance, Jared turned to see what the ruckus was all about. All he saw, though, was a small flurry of paper falling to the ground.

Squirrels screeched and birds scattered as Ghoulie pursued the cartoon crook deep into the woods. Through underbrush, over and under fallen logs they ran, until Ghoulie tackled Beamer, plunging with him through a tall thicket.

"What are you doing?" he shouted as he sat on Beamer's chest.

"You can't do it!" Beamer grunted, tightly clutching the notebook. "Not with this!"

Finally, Scilla charged up to them. "Hey you two!" she yelled as she pulled Ghoulie off of Beamer. "Cut it out!"

"It's not right," Beamer gasped as he wiped the dirt from his face. "You can't threaten somebody with something they do good. It's not right!"

"But this is *Jared* we're talkin' about! It's the only way—"

"There's got to be some other way!" Beamer said as he scrambled to his feet.

"Beamer," Ghoulie complained, pacing in a little circle, "we finally get a chance to …"

Ghoulie stopped pacing and gave Beamer a long look. Finally, his shoulders slumped and he plopped down atop a fallen tree trunk. "Look, I know. I've had it done to me all my life. But just once I'd like to give a little back!"

"You haven't lived long enough for 'all my life'!" said Beamer with half a grin. His voice softened. "If it's not right when it's done to us, it's not right for us to do it to Jared," Beamer said. "This," he said, holding out a drawing, "is a gift—a gift from God, not a weakness—whether he knows it or not."

"All right, all right," Ghoulie sighed finally, "I just hope he's got more than one Achilles' heel."

*　*　*　*　*

At that moment Jared was where the others had left the trail a few minutes earlier, staring at a crumpled cartoon drawing. His face was as hard as granite. Something was going on. These guys were messing around in his business.

He shifted his mind into bash'em-and-trash'em overdrive. Drawing was his private thing. Nobody was supposed to know … Nobody! It wasn't cool. Kids would laugh. They had three years ago, when he'd lived in Molterville. Since then, he'd shot up a foot and moved, but he'd made himself a solemn promise that nobody would ever laugh at him again.

Jared was now determined to finish the job he had started a year ago when something in that tree—he couldn't remember what—had stopped him. *Those—what did they call themselves? Ah, right, Star-Fighters. Those Star-Fighters and their weird tree house would soon be history—ancient and in ruins.* Beamer and Ghoulie didn't belong in Jared's world. If they

refused to scurry away before him, he would simply
have to squash them … like bugs.

15
Freak Storm

A few minutes later Beamer, Ghoulie, and Scilla pushed through a wall of bushes heading back toward the main path.

"C'mon," said Ghoulie impatiently. "I'll be late!"

Scilla turned to Beamer and said mischievously, "I found out how you got the name Beamer."

Beamer whirled about, ready for a fight. "Who told you? Did my brother—?"

"No, my grandma heard it from your mom."

"Aw ... come on, Beamer," Ghoulie goaded him. "Out with it, Scilla."

"Grandma said that when Beamer was little, he always watched old *Star Trek* episodes with his dad."

"Scillaaaa ..." Beamer growled.

"He'd laugh when people would sizzle away on the transporter pad after they said, 'Beam me up, Scottie.' So they called him Beamer."

"Well, it beats Scilla!" Beamer shot back at her. "Scilla sounds like somethin' a doctor shoots into you with a needle."

"It does not!" she yelled as she jabbed him with her fist. "Take that back, or I'll start calling your real name out loud during recess!"

"You do and I'll—" Beamer yelled, fighting off a flurry of fists.

"Benson! Benson! Benson!" she taunted.

"Wait a minute! Wait a minute!" Ghoulie said, as they

came back to where they had left the path. He began searching around the area. "Didn't we drop a couple of drawings around here somewhere?"

"You're right!" said Beamer, flipping through the sheets he'd stuffed into Jared's notebook. "Maybe they blew away." In truth, the wind was beginning to pick up.

Feeling a pit forming in his stomach, Beamer's search became more frantic. "We've gotta find them! I've got a very bad feeling about this."

But the wind was churning up the forest, whipping leaves and brush into their eyes.

"Hey, guys!" Ghoulie yelled, looking up at the sky. Clouds were swooping over the tree tops, churning and boiling as if they had a life of their own. It was suddenly very dark and cold.

Then they heard something strange—like static when the cable TV gets knocked out. The tall buildings and hills in the distance seemed to be hidden behind a white fog.

"C'mon, let's get home," Ghoulie said. They started off in a loping trot, glancing furtively over their shoulder at the ominous cloud bank. The crackling sound grew louder. Soon they were running.

When they shot out into the open area of the park, the distance to home seemed like miles. "The shortcut!" Scilla cried. "Let's take the shortcut. We'll never make it around Parkview."

"No way," Beamer answered, shaking his head firmly. "I don't want anything to do with that place."

Suddenly a blast of cold wind nearly drove them to the ground. Something began to fall—gently at first, but there was a sharp sting with every pitter-pat.

"Come on, Beamer," Ghoulie insisted anxiously. "We got through all right last time."

Reluctantly Beamer changed course and followed. With the wind at their backs, they practically flew through the bushes toward the wall. Then the sky burst open.

A torrent of tiny ice pellets pummeled them like machine gun fire. It was Noah's deluge in ice. Hail, to be more precise, coming down in waves and stinging like a zillion mosquito bites. By the time they reached the wall, the ground was already white with crunchy "snow."

They dived into the tunnel beneath the wall and scrambled through the cavern and up the rock steps. Soon they were scurrying through the fantasy-land garden. Halfway to the gate, the castle lights blinked out. Each dark window now looked like a gaping mouth.

The hail coating the ground was two inches deep and growing thicker by the second when Beamer yanked the gate handle. It didn't move. "Hey!" he shouted and tried it again.

"Hurry up, Beamer!" Scilla cried out, squeezing in to force the handle.

"What is it, stuck?" asked Ghoulie, who had pulled his jacket up over his head.

"No," Beamer replied. "It's locked ... tight. Somebody has fixed the gate!"

Lightning ripped open the sky and the hail came down even harder. "Yiiii!!" they yelped, crowding their already snow-coated bodies tightly against the house.

A sharp rapping sound spun them around. Beamer instinctively recoiled. A stern figure holding an oil lamp

loomed in the window above them. It was her—Old
Lady Parker, in the flesh!

16

Castle Quest and No Pants

Her face masked by dark shadows, the old woman gestured stiffly toward the back of the house. Another burst of lightning reflected brightly in the window. Then the window was dark and empty.

Realizing they had no choice, they meekly shuffled along the wall, cringing beneath the force of the hail, until a door creaked and swung open in their faces.

"Come on now," said a maid holding a candle. "Get in here before you catch something dangerous."

"Yes, Ma'am," Scilla said with a gulp. They all nodded sheepishly and clattered up the steps.

"And don't forget to wipe your feet," she added firmly, pointing to the mat. "We don't want you trackin' the whole neighborhood inside." Her voice was almost musical, each syllable a different note. Beamer checked through his movie memory banks and concluded she was probably Irish or Swedish or something.

As the door closed behind them, the house lights suddenly came back on.

"Well, now, that didn't take long." The maid sighed and blew out the candle.

They were in the laundry room, clearly once a screened-in porch about the size of a long, narrow bedroom.

Beamer started to step into the adjoining kitchen when the maid called, "Hold on there! You're sopping wet with that stuff meltin' off ya. I don't want to have to clean up more than one room." She shuffled through a pile of large, newly washed towels.

"Here," she said, handing one to each of them. "Dry yourself off. Come to think of it, you'd better take these things off," she said, fingering Beamer's soaked sleeve.

"But I live just down the street!" Beamer protested.

"Maybe so, but there's no way Ms. Parker will hear of me sendin' ya back out into a downpour like this. So get those clothes off. I'll stick 'em in the dryer and they'll be dry in no time. You can wrap another towel around you while ya wait."

Beamer and Ghoulie looked at each other, then at Scilla. Suddenly the maid realized the problem. "Oh, my ... of course," she said apologetically. "Sorry, deary. In your present state I didn't realize what ... ah ... who you were." She giggled in a high-pitched squeal, then reached out and wrapped Scilla in a towel. "Here, you can come with me. I'll take care of you." As the maid ushered her through the kitchen and out the far door, Scilla looked back at Beamer and Ghoulie as if she were being marched off to a firing squad.

"If we're gonna get out of here," Ghoulie said, fumbling with the door latch, "it had better be now. Our whole lives could be ruined if we have to escape without pants."

"Hey! We can't leave Scilla here alone!" Beamer said, pulling him back into the room.

"What makes you think we'll ever see Scilla again?" Ghoulie croaked.

Beamer gave him a wry grin and started unbuttoning his shirt.

The maid returned minutes later to find the boys wrapped in towels like Sitting Bull at a powwow. Seeing their clothes strewn across the floor, she shook her head and placed her hands on her hips. "Boys ... I should have remembered. Come with me," she said with a sigh.

The boys looked at each other, swallowed hard, and followed her through the kitchen. Its old-world look was not what it seemed. Neatly disguised within the prehistoric brick walls and amidst the copper cookware were microwave ovens, electric openers, compactors, giant mixers, and a huge double-door refrigerator built into the wall—the latest high-tech gadgets in cooking.

They passed through an octagonal dining room; three walls were filled with windows, one with a fireplace, and the rest with sparkling dishes and paintings. Finally they were in the main hallway walking toward a huge double front door of stained glass. The temptation to bolt for it was strong; then the maid whisked them around to climb the staircase. Beamer gave a last wistful look over his shoulder as the door grew lower and smaller behind them.

The lady led them up one story, then up two more before turning down a dark, wide hallway toward the front of the house. Light leaked through the slats in the louvered doors directly ahead. The maid swung them open. Inside, someone gasped and whirled around to face them. It was Scilla, looking like Pocahontas in an oversized robe. Seeing them, she sighed in relief and tightened the robe around her.

"You can all wait here in the sitting room," the maid said, pulling the doors closed. "And don't touch a thing!" she added, popping her head back in momentarily.

"Does that mean we can't sit down?" Ghoulie asked, looking about the room.

"Of course you can sit," Scilla said, rolling her eyes. "She said it was a sitting room."

That was about the only thing the room was good for—sitting. There were books, chairs, small tables, several bookcases, and lots of glass figures, but little else—not a

TV, game machine, or computer in sight. In spite of the dark woodwork, half a dozen lamps gave the room a warm glow.

"Somebody around here goes in big-time for readin'," Scilla remarked, looking over the large, carved bookcase which filled one wall. "Isn't reading supposed to be bad for your eyes?"

"Only if you read under the covers at night with a flashlight," Ghoulie said with a shrug. "Anyway, that's what my nanny told me when I tried it."

A rush of snow pelting the window brought them around. The hailstorm had turned into a blizzard.

This was a major wall of glass—a huge bay window with ten-foot-high side panels angled in at 45 degrees and made up of a checkerboard of square, cut-glass panes. At the moment, however, it was powdered with pockets of snow and rattling in the wind.

"Wow, would you look at that!" Scilla exclaimed.

Murphy Street—trees, rooftops, and all—was white with snow. What was funny, though, was that the trees and rooftops two streets over had no snow on them.

Leaving Beamer still gazing out the window, Ghoulie and Scilla bounded into big, stuffed chairs on either side of a lamp table facing the fireplace. Scilla bounced around in hers, checking out the springs, and then leaned forward.

"Hey, look at these," she said, noticing the glass-door book-cases built in around the fireplace. She hopped out of her chair and approached them. Fingering the cut-glass door, she looked inside at the colorful gold- and silver-lettered books. "These are the fanciest books I've ever seen!" She pulled the delicate door-knob of the cabinet as Ghoulie came up beside her.

"Rats!" she said. The door was locked. "Wait a minute," she said, noticing a glass door on the other side of the fireplace that wasn't completely closed.

She opened the door and pulled out a book that was lying on its side. "Oooh, this one's really cool," she said, sucking in her breath. There were squiggled gold designs all over the cover. "R.I.P.," Scilla said, reading the biggest designs in the middle. "Who would ever name a book Rest in Peace?" she exclaimed.

She tried to open it. "Hey, it's locked!"

"Locked?" Beamer said, turning from the window. "Whoever heard of a locked book? Most of the time everybody's trying to get you to open a book, not lock you out." He came over for a closer look.

"It must have a key, then," Scilla said. "I bet it's right around here someplace." They looked on the lamp tables and in a candy dish. Scilla was too short to see what was on top of the mantle, but she brushed her hands along it, feeling for the key. "Hey, what's this?" she asked when she swept something metallic to the edge of the mantle. She reached for it but fumbled it to the floor where it clanged on the tile at the base of the fireplace.

Beamer quickly scooped it up. Even more quickly, Scilla snatched the key out of his hand and grabbed the book out of Ghoulie's at the same time. "Let's try it," she said, placing the book on the table between the two fireplace chairs.

She carefully inserted the key and turned it. With a slight click the leather flap fell loose. "It worked!" she exclaimed in a hushed voice. She opened it reverently. "Hey, it's not printed!" she gulped. "It's somebody's handwriting." She flipped back to the front page. There, in bold letters, was written, "The Diary of Rebecca Ilene Parker."

"D'you mean, R.I.P. is Old Lady Parker's name?" Beamer said as he reached over to flip through the pages. "She used to crawl through that tunnel?"

"We can't look at this," Scilla gasped, starting to close it.

"Hey, look," Beamer interrupted. "There's something about the meteor!" He pushed in closer.

"No, it's bad luck to read somebody else's diary!" Scilla insisted, trying to wrest the book away from him.

"Wait a minute!" Beamer insisted. "She's talking about the tree—our tree! See!" he exclaimed, jabbing his finger at the words: " ... the night the meteor struck."

"Cool!" Scilla whispered in awe.

"What meteor?" Ghoulie asked in confusion.

"Listen!" Beamer began to read: "This was a different kind of storm. The night was clear and glowing with stars until the sky flashed with the light of a meteor shower. I saw one streak of fire slice through the night and split in half a tree down the street. Flames leaped up, then quickly faded. I don't know why. It had rained earlier, so maybe it was too wet to burn."

He paused, turning the page to the next day's entry. He continued: "I went over to look at the tree today. It was black all over and completely split in two, but there were still little green buds all over it. It couldn't live after that, could it?"

"You were told to touch nothing!" a deep, crackling voice thundered behind them.

17

Legend

"Old" didn't begin to describe Old Lady Parker! This lady of the castle had wrinkles where no wrinkles had been before. She used a cane, but frail she wasn't. In fact, she was big enough to have been Arnold Schwarzenegger's grand-mother.

"Young lady," she said in an icy voice, "please bring that book to me."

Scilla handed the old woman the book, still open to the page they had been reading. "We saw that you were writing about the tree and—" Scilla said weakly.

"Silence!" the woman ordered.

"It's my fault," Beamer stammered. "Scilla tried to close the book back up when she saw it was a diary, but I saw that about the tree and, well, I just had to know—"

"Yes, I see," she interrupted him, looking down at the page. She closed the book and latched it. "You must learn to balance what *you* want with respect for the property of others." She spoke with a husky voice that was somehow deep and strong but quiet at the same time.

"Yes, Ma'am." They all nodded together like a church choir.

"I recognize that I am partly to blame," Ms. Parker stated

as she returned the book to its shelf. "I was in such a hurry to find a lamp when the lights went out that I failed to return the book to its proper place." She locked the glass door and turned back to them.

Looking from one to the other, she seemed to be sizing them up in a way that was downright unnerving. "So you are the children who are playing in the tree house these days."

They all nodded their heads at once, with a stream of "uh-huhs."

"Not just anyone can play in that tree house, you know. Those with malice in their hearts have always found the experience to be ... nightmarish. I don't know how or why."

She paused a moment, then continued, "So, I can assume you have no malice?"

They shook their heads from side to side simultaneously, with a chorus of "huh-uhs."

"Go ahead, sit back down," she gestured to them abruptly. They did so without taking their eyes off her. The thud of her cane on the wooden floor made a strange beat with her shuffling steps. "How much do you know about the meteor?"

"I ...," stammered Beamer, "I saw it on display in the museum, but it didn't say it split the tree in half."

"I've seen it too," said Ghoulie. "It's just an ugly old rock."

"Yes, you're right, of course," Ms. Parker croaked. "But things can be more than they seem. Do you have any idea how many wishes were spent on that rock during the short time it flashed through the sky back in the spring of 1919?"

"Well, no," Ghoulie mumbled with a shrug. "They're just wishes ... superstitions. Nothing ever comes of them."

"Yeah," muttered Beamer. "I wished on one the day we

moved in, but it didn't do any good." He plopped back into his chair. "We're still here. My wish didn't come true—not even close."

"I wouldn't be so sure, if I were you," the aged woman said, pointing her cane first at Ghoulie, then at Beamer. "Wishes are not for the fainthearted. A wish, you see," she went on as she slowly moved toward them, "is a piece of a dream. And a dream—oh, not one of those little nighttime wisps that flee when you wake up, but the kind that stick with you by day as well as night—a dream is very powerful. Maybe the most powerful force on earth."

"Oh, brother," Ghoulie muttered to Scilla. "It's a rock, not plutonium."

"My hearing's very good, young man," Ms. Parker said as she turned back toward the shamefaced boy. "Come here. I want to show you something."

Ghoulie slid from his chair, swallowing hard, and walked hesitantly toward her.

As he approached, she held out her hand, palm down. "What do you see there?" she asked.

Ghoulie's eyes became enormous, as only Ghoulie's could. "A diamond!" he gasped. "The biggest one I ever heard of."

Beamer and Scilla leaped from their chairs and crowded in beside him, straining to see. True enough, the ring on her finger held a glittering stone bigger than a marble shooter.

"No, it's just a rock," she corrected him. She moved toward the window, her cane making a clopping beat on the floor with every other step. "Without dreams, you see, clay would be dirt instead of bricks and buildings; oil would be nothing more than a smelly, black bog; and electricity, only a loud, jagged streak in the sky."

As if on cue, lightning flashed once more, illuminating the

tree ship. "Billy Stoller built that tree house," she said, peering thoughtfully at it. "He was thirteen years old, and the tree was one of the smaller ones in what was a vacant lot back then. His father wanted to use a bigger tree, not one twisted and broken. But that tree had been singled out by a falling star, and Billy Stoller would build his spaceship in no other.

"You see, Billy Stoller dreamed about traveling to the stars. Almost nobody dreamed of such things back then. But Billy took his dream and made a spaceship in a tree. I thought he was weird and laughed at him. I called him the worst possible names," she added with a chuckle. "He might as well have had bug eyes and antennae, as far as I was concerned.

"Anyway, he'd puff up red and mad but kept right at his dream. Ten years later, when he began teaching at the college, he built that house on the lot. And not too many years after that he helped Mr. Goddard build his first rockets.

"You have to be special to have a dream like that. You see, ordinary people—people like me," she chuckled, "don't understand that God can make some people different—special—for a reason.

"People with big dreams have lived and played on this street ever since." She walked up smack in front of Beamer and gave him a penetrating look. "Maybe your dream isn't big enough. And maybe your wish was too small. Have you ever thought of that, young man?"

With her looming above him like a thundercloud, Beamer couldn't get his jaw to work.

"Yes," she continued, turning back to the others, "when that meteor struck, it was like the finger of God touched the earth right here on Murphy Street. And something indescribable spread out from that spot like a ripple in a pond."

Her eyes took on a misty look. "I don't know that you have to come to Murphy Street to get that touch. I suspect that there are other streets like this one and, for that matter, that God can touch every person if it's in their hearts to accept that touch. But, as for Murphy Street, well, three Nobel Prize winners, four Pulitzer winners, a number of world-class artists and musicians, not to mention a pretty fair cartoonist, grew up here."

"And at least one big-time cobweb architect," muttered Beamer.

"And a lot of very good people who made a big difference one time or another in otherwise normal, everyday lives ... not bad for a street one block long," Ms. Parker continued.

"When you see those cracks in the sidewalk down there ..." She paused, and then continued. "Think about those children who came before you, who scraped their knees and climbed that tree just like you do now and made their dreams real."

She looked them over critically, and then made her way haltingly toward the doorway. "We shall see what you make of yours." Then, without looking back, she lumbered out the door in a whisper of shifting silk.

* * * * *

The storm stopped as suddenly as it began. And, amazingly, Old Lady Parker did let them go home, dry and in neatly pressed clothes.

Strangely enough, the icy snow had fallen on only one side of the park and a few blocks beyond. Murphy Street was right in the middle. The next day, Friday, newspapers were filled with stories about the freak storm. A couple of schools in the affected area, including the middle school, were closed as a result, so Beamer and the Star-Fighters got the day off to build snowmen. When they were through, though, they were surprised to see that their trio of snow figures looked like pudgy versions of Jared and his goons.

It didn't bother them quite so much anymore that they were different. After all, being special was what Murphy Street seemed to be all about. Even the idea of being "alien" was beginning to have a nice ring to it; although they'd just as soon some kids wouldn't look at them like they were French fries in need of catsup.

And that, of course, was the problem. Jared was up to something. They could feel it like thunder in the distance. Right now would be a good time for whatever made them special to kick in with some brilliant plan.

18

War Games

The season wasn't really ready yet for snow, so, by the end of the day, it was mostly melted. Ghoulie got permission to sleep over with Beamer; but your typical sleepover it wasn't. Mom and Dad couldn't figure it out—no Xbox, no shaving cream fights, no monster flicks. They had dinner and then watched E.T.'s death scene seven times.

They even went to bed early. Then, instead of exchanging ghost stories, they just lay there in the dark, staring up at the ceiling.

"You know what our problem is, don't you?" Ghoulie said.

"What?" Beamer said.

"We have more Achilles' heels than Jared does."

"Yeah, that's for sure," Beamer sighed.

They lay there silently for awhile, then Beamer started crying ... or was it laughing?

"One thing about being pulverized ...," Beamer chortled after a few moments.

"What's that?" Ghoulie asked with a smirk.

" ... We won't have to untie our shoes to get them off," Beamer finished with a snuffled laugh.

"Nice try, MacIntyre," Ghoulie drawled. "If you think of a way to make Jared laugh to death, let me know."

"Jared doesn't laugh at funny," Beamer said, still snickering. "Only at mean."

"Right, I forgot," Ghoulie said wryly. "Laughter's the only thing he's afraid of—people laughing at him, that is."

Beamer's snuffled laughter faded into silence. A germ of an

idea began to form in his mind. Suddenly he rolled over and sat up. "That's it!" he shouted. "That's his Achilles' heel!"

"MacIntyre," Ghoulie groaned, "haven't we had enough of heels for awhile?"

"So, whadda we got to lose?" Beamer demanded, jumping out of bed. "If we can get him into something so funny that everybody'll split their guts laughing—"

"How are we going to do that?" Ghoulie inquired, reluctantly sitting up. "Bozo the Clown is dead, and Ronald MacDonald's not available, and in no way does Jared resemble either one of them."

"But that's not—" Beamer tried to interrupt.

"And suppose we could set him up," Ghoulie kept on. "We'd have to get him in front of an audience, which would be about as easy as getting Mount Rushmore to Nashville. Not to mention, we'd become worm meat for the effort."

"We're already worm meat," Beamer shot back, "but if we make it happen when and where and how *we* choose, then . . ."

" . . . We can turn Jared's homicidal tendencies into comedy?" Ghoulie finished for him doubtfully. "Man, you really are a dreamer."

"Can you get one of your dad's other video cameras Saturday morning?" Beamer said, pacing the floor in excitement.

"Yeah . . . ," he responded, suddenly getting the drift of Beamer's idea.

"Listen, Scilla said that Jared cuts through the park every Saturday to go to the afternoon movie, right?"

"Uh, I think so . . . yeah, right. But that's soon!"

"That's probably all the time we've got left!"

A few minutes later Beamer and Ghoulie were cutting through the attic en route to the tree ship. Beamer had to practically drag Ghoulie past the web. Actually, Beamer wasn't too keen on it himself, the way it glowed eerie silver in the moonbeam.

Climbing through the tall windows, they crept across the shingled roof to the big tree branch which overhung the house.

Ghoulie stopped just before he was ready to step from the roof to the tree. "Did you hear what your sister said at dinner?" he said, eyeing the tree curiously.

"No, listening to her has been known to cause brain damage," said Beamer with a smirk.

"Well, she was just repeating what that scientist guy she follows around said."

"Oh man, not him!"

"He's found an energy field around the tree—bigger than the one around the web! But get this: they're connected, passing energy back and forth between them."

"My sister said that? She doesn't know a field from a hair brush."

"Well, she didn't say it quite that way. I had to do a little translation."

"Do you think that's why we go off to other galaxies in our heads?"

"I don't know. I'm thinking about it."

It was warm, like Indian summer, and the music of night life was all around them as they climbed through the tangle of branches. The night was bright, even though the sky was mostly clouded over. A circular opening around the full moon made it look like a giant eye in the sky.

"Hey, wait a minute," Beamer said, catching a glint from something in the tree. He looked closer, then slowly reached

inside his old friend the squirrel's home toward whatever
it was. What he came out with was that shiny dark object
Beamer had seen the squirrel carrying around months ago.
Beamer held it up in the moonlight and turned it around and
around.

"The meteor!" he suddenly blurted.

"What are you talking about?" Ghoulie asked, scrunching
up close to peer over his shoulder.

"This is the missing chip from the meteor in the museum."

"Come on, Beamer, it's just a rock," Ghoulie muttered, as
he moved on up the tree.

"That's what you said to Ms. Parker. Ghoulie, this is it. I'm
sure of it!"

"Okay, okay, so you've got a piece of a meteor for your very
own," Ghoulie said, still uninterested.

"No, it's more than that. It's a piece of a falling star, a star
that hit *my* tree, Ghoulie—*my* tree!"

"Sure, Beamer. Now would you hurry and get up here,"
Ghoulie ordered impatiently.

"D'ya know what I think? The energy field came from the
meteor. It had some kind of radiation so that when it blasted
the tree, it gave it some kind of ... something. The squirrel
... or maybe its ancestor all those years ago," Beamer went
on talking to the air, "must have mistaken it for an acorn and
taken it up to its nest."

Beamer pocketed his new treasure and reached back in the
hollow to pick up a handful of acorns. "We're gonna need all
the help we can get. I'll pay ya' back later," he said to the invis-
ible squirrel, and then he began to throw the nuts, one by one,
at Scilla's window. Finally it opened and Scilla's irritated face
poked out.

"Hey, what's it take for a girl to get a little sleep around here?" she asked with a gigantic yawn.

"Meet us in the ship," Beamer whispered loudly. "We've got work to do."

"Now? Are you crazy?" she exclaimed.

"It's now or never, and I mean *never*."

She gave him a long look. "I'll be right over."

* * * * *

A little after five o'clock on Saturday afternoon, Jared and four other boys were on their bicycles, weaving in and out of traffic. Anyone within ten blocks would have known where they were from the sound of horns blaring. Usually only Jeffries and Slocum went with Jared to the Saturday movie. Today, though, was special. Today, there was going to be a war.

The movie—*Mean Streets Aflame*—couldn't have been better chosen to pump them up for the massacre ahead. Yes, "Operation Demolition" was underway. You see, bad guys make plans too. Before Beamer even had a glimmer of an idea, Jared had already laid out his hit plan. Like a teen Mafia kingpin, he'd gathered all the facts; he'd analyzed his enemies—their abilities and limitations, who would be where, when—and predicted their means of retaliation.

In one swift attack, Jared was going to bring them to their knees ... forever.

* * * * *

Beamer and Ghoulie were waiting at the far end of the park where the largest of the forest paths opened up into a broad playing field.

"Now I know what it feels like to be a guppy," groaned

Ghoulie, propping his head on top of his bicycle handlebars. He fingered nervously the strap to a small video camera that was slung around his neck.

"How else are we going to get him into the backyard?" Beamer explained for the seventeenth time.

"Being bait for a shark is not what I had in mind!"

"All we gotta do is make sure we don't let him get too close."

They sat quietly on their bikes, anxiously looking up the trail. The wind rippled their clothes, tugging at the hood of Ghoulie's sweatjacket. A sky full of big, puffy clouds made the park a patchwork of green and shadow.

"What's taking them so long?" Ghoulie finally broke the silence.

"I don't know," Beamer shrugged. "Maybe the movie went long."

"But we got the time for the next showing, remember?"

"Yeah, okay ... well, then ... could be they stopped for a Coke or a video game or something. I don't know."

Ghoulie turned to wipe his nose on his sleeve, then lost his breath in a world-class *gasp*! Beamer turned around to see what the matter was, and saw Ghoulie's eyes growing to roughly the size of poached eggs. He followed the direction of Ghoulie's shaking finger.

19

Invasion!

There they were—the bad news troop—in full force, coming from the wrong direction and going the wrong way. The Star-Fighters had been outflanked, outfoxed, out-maneuvered, and were definitely out-manned. Just like that, Beamer's plan was blown to pieces.

"Well, we'll just have to try again next Saturday," Beamer said, trying to shrug it off.

Then the full extent of the disaster blew over them like a nuclear shock wave. Just when Jared's goon squad should have zigged *left* for home, they zigged *right*!

"I don't like the looks of this," Beamer murmured, a lump forming in his throat. "They're headed for Murphy Street." Then he saw it—the crooked fan tail of a crowbar sticking out of Jared's saddle bag.

"Oh no!" Beamer gasped as he watched them round a turn onto Murphy Street. "They're headed for the house!" he cried.

Beamer and Ghoulie peeled out at near light speed, but there was a major pit where Beamer's stomach should have been. Not even warp drive was going to get them home ahead of Jared. And Scilla was there alone!

Yep, Jared couldn't have timed it better if he'd been able to read their minds. Erin was at cheerleader tryouts and Michael was with Dad and Mom, who were working at the school rummage sale.

Beamer pedaled like his life depended upon it, shaking his head in dismay. Right now, the battle for the tree ship had all the earmarks of a middle-school Armageddon.

* * * * *

One thing was in Scilla's favor: She didn't have time to worry about it. Perched in her treetop lookout position, she was watching for Beamer and Ghoulie to come tearing around the corner into Murphy Street, with Jared and gang in hot pursuit. The only trouble she'd had so far was from birds. A whole flock of tiny, noisy black birds heading south had settled in their tree for a rest stop. Her grandma called them starlings. In fact, it took her a minute to realize that the new noise at the bottom of the tree wasn't coming from them.

"All right," she suddenly heard a voice snarl from below. "Looks like we caught 'em with their pants down. Let's make this quick and messy."

Scilla nearly fell out of her perch. *Where are Beamer and Ghoulie?*

"Do we have to carry up the sledgehammer?" Slocum whined.

"Holy tamole!" Scilla mouthed silently. In desperation, she quietly slipped and tripped and sometimes fell, branch by branch, down toward the tree ship.

Jared and his gang hadn't spotted her yet.

"Yeah, take it," Jared growled. "We don't want anything left of their precious tree house but splinters." Slocum groaned and tucked the sledgehammer in his belt.

As Jared vaulted onto the slanted trunk, Scilla landed, rump first, on the ramp. "Just like a bunch of boys to leave a girl to do their dirty work," she muttered as she pushed painfully to her feet. *This isn't even my fight. Maybe I could just hide in the leaves until they leave.*

When Jared got where the slanted trunk turned and climbed more straight up, he stopped, suddenly uneasy. "You guys go first," he called behind. "I'll take ... uh ... an anchor position ... in case the dorks show up and are stupid enough to follow us up the tree."

Seemingly satisfied with this thin explanation, Jared's clones scrambled past him and on up into the branches, thickly cloaked with dark red leaves. Jared could see snatches of the bullet-shaped structure, newly painted and gleaming. What bothered him was the not-quite-blocked-out memory of the last time he had climbed this tree. But that time he had been alone. Now he was here in force. He took a deep breath, tucked his crowbar into his belt, and again started to climb.

Scilla quickly shut and barred the tree ship's door behind her. She looked at the plywood control panels, her eyes again flaring in panic. There were supposed to be three pair of hands working the controls, not just one. She paced back and forth like an anxious penguin trying to decide what to do first.

Then, just as if someone had flipped a switch, she was Lieutenant Bruzelski again and everything popped into focus. Why she was alone on the scout vessel, she couldn't say, but she knew her duty. "Screen on — mark zero, zero, zero!" she announced authoritatively, her hands playing across the dials. Immediately the view screen flickered on and, with it, the camera. "Yes!" she exclaimed, seeing the view angle shift to focus directly on the area below the ship.

There they were, Jeffries and Slocum, along with two others, Phillips and Johnson. At least that's who she thought they were. She blinked to clear her eyes, then took another look. To her Lieutenant Bruzelski eyes, these were entirely different creatures — creatures from a world alien to her own. The one Scilla had thought was Slocum now had gills that flared every time he took a breath and a large floppy fin at the top of his head which kept falling into his eyes. Jeffries got stuck with the bug eyes and antennae and what may or may not have been a mustache. The other two had pig heads with big slavering lips, floppy ears, and pimples.

"Releasing atmospheric distortion field!" Officer Bruzelski said with the ease of a practiced defender. Immediately the ship ejected a cloud of hydrogen oxide — water, that is — from a line of lawn sprinklers they had strung in the branches.

"*Eeowww! Hey*!" four voices shrieked at once.

"*Aiiiieeeee!*" cried the fifth. It was Jeffries, who had stared, point-blank, into a sprinkler head just as it went off. He took a free fall backward into a wide web of branches below him.

"They're up there!" Slocum yelled.

"All right, spread out." Jared ordered. "Nobody ever got sprinkled to death." He laughed and they joined in with him, all except for Jeffries, that is, who was nursing a hundred scrapes and scratches.

Now Bruzelski could see what should have been Jared. His ears were huge, like big fans sticking straight out from either side of his head. Instead of a mouth, he had mandibles, so that he seemed to be talking sideways. On top of his head was a huge plume like a rooster's.

Calmly, with a precision born of strict training at Sector Four Space Academy, Lieutenant Bruzelski moved to her next line of defense. "Activating stickeyon emission controls," she said as she ran from panel to bleeping panel.

Nothing happened ... or so it seemed.

Then Slocum, who was now in the lead, reached up for a higher branch and felt something strange.

20

Nightmare on Murphy Street

"Hey!" Slocum grunted as he looked at the black, gooey mess on his hand. He sniffed, then licked it. It was sweet. "J-a-a-a-r-eh-eh-d?" he yelled down to his boss, then took another lick.

"What?" Jared shouted back impatiently.

At the same time, Jeffries reached up for a grip. Both hands, instead, grabbed a handful of slimy gook and slipped. "*Aiiiiiiii!*" he screamed as he fell for the second time back into the prickly cradle of branches.

The gooey mess poured down the trunk like a heavy coat of paint, engulfing hands and feet, dribbling into mouths and over eyes.

"Hey! Eeeeeee! Yecchh! Whoaaah! Jaaar-ed!" came a chorus of yelps and screeches.

The slippery gook was, in fact, molasses from those old barrels in the garage—the ones Dr. Mac had been trying to cook back into lip-smacking goodness.

"Spread out away from the trunk," Jared shouted to his henchmen, backing away as the gook glided down toward him. "Climb up one branch at a time."

Muttering unmentionables, his troops shuffled out on their respective limbs and began hoisting themselves up, branch by branch.

Almost immediately, though, Phillips reached up for a handhold and tipped over something. A wide curtain of molasses rained down on him. "*Eeeeiii,*" he yowled like a cat who had fallen into a puddle, and fell backward, ending up hanging upside down with his legs wrapped around a branch. "J-a-a-r-eh-eh-d!" he cried bitterly.

Jared looked up just in time to get a face-full of the splashdown.

Seeing Jared's face, Slocum, on the other side of the trunk, couldn't hold back a snicker.

Jared glared murderously at him as he wiped the glop from his eyes.

Sobering quickly, Slocum reached up ... and tipped over a long tray-full of his own.

The Star-Fighters had set up gutter sections, left over from Dr. Mac's home improvement project, all over the tree, and had filled them with molasses.

Jared's gloppidy-glop crew was livid, uttering words nobody nice ever used in the English language.

"Come on, you cowards!" Jared roared, grabbing Jeffries as he slid by. "You back down because of some pancake syrup and you'll be the joke of the school!"

It was then that Beamer and Ghoulie finally skidded into the yard, dismounting even before they stopped.

Ghoulie took off for the tree, only to have his feet slip out from under him in mid-run. "Yeooow!" he howled as he skidded into a dark, sticky puddle.

Beamer held a finger-full of the dark gook to his nose. "They're up there, all right, and Scilla's on the counterattack."

"Hey—!" Ghoulie started to shout up to Scilla when Beamer suddenly clapped his hand tightly over Ghoulie's mouth.

"Sshhh," he whispered urgently. "You don't want them to come down, do you? *We* don't have any defenses. *She* does."

Ghoulie shuddered just thinking about it.

"I've got an idea," Beamer whispered as he ran to the door of the house. "Come on."

They streaked inside, Beamer reaching to catch the screen door a moment before it slammed closed.

In spite of Lieutenant Bruzelski's valiant efforts, the syrupy slime bags were still coming.

"Firing Veton Depth charges!" she announced, pulling down hard on a lever.

This time a line of popguns shot what looked like Ping Pong balls into the air. As they struck the surrounding branches they broke open, making a sound like popcorn popping and making it rain, not molasses, but birdseed—barrage after barrage of birdseed—a dust storm of little grains that found a nice, sticky home aboard the hapless, molasses-drenched crew below.

"Hey! What is—? Who—Man! I'll get him!" five angry voices cried out, suddenly finding themselves coated with tiny yellow and white particles.

But the worst was yet to come, though it was totally unplanned. All those gaggling birds that had been driving Scilla crazy before caught one whiff of that molasses and birdseed and, well, suddenly discovered five giant, yummy bird feeders ready for the pecking. There was the racket of dozens of flapping wings on the move.

The boys yelled, swatting furiously at the hungry birds while trying to hang on to the tree at the same time.

One boy, Johnson, *did* fall—all the way down into Dr. Mac's safety net. Completely panicked, he scrambled across the net and fell to the ground. The seed-coated boy scurried and crunched off, gasping for breath, with a flock of tiny birds twisting and turning on his tail.

Back in the tree, the frantic cries and swatting hands of the Skullcross Gang finally succeeded in sending the hungry birds away in a black cloud that swirled up and around the tree then away southward. Breathing hard, soaked with water, coated with molasses and peppered with birdseed, Jared was beyond cussing. He pulled himself along a branch to beneath the tree ship's entry ramp and hoisted himself up. There he was, staring across the ramp toward the tree ship's door, his chest heaving with anger.

With the noise of the birds gone, Jared now began to feel and hear what sounded like the wind. For a moment, he looked anxious, uncertain.

Up in the attic, Beamer and Ghoulie were feeling pretty uncertain themselves.

"Oh, man, look at that," Beamer said in a hushed voice, as they stared at the web. It was a brilliant yellow-white, almost too bright to look at. The instruments surrounding the web were all registering readings at the limit of their range.

"I think your attic is about to take off!" Ghoulie exclaimed. "The web must be picking up energy from the tree."

"How can it do that?" Beamer asked. "Spiders don't have electro—whatever, do they?" *Just what the world needs—a high-tech spider invasion!*

"Good question," said Ghoulie. "The last I heard, the stuff that mostly makes up spiderwebs isn't supposed to conduct electricity."

But if a spider didn't make the web, who did—and why? Murphy Street definitely had way more mysteries than one little street had a right to. Beamer shook his head to clear it.

"We don't have time to figure this out now!" yelled Beamer. He didn't know why he yelled, because the web made no sound. "We have to get to the tree ship!"

They made their way through an opening in the web and climbed out the window. They could hear the noise of battle.

Jeffries, Slocum, and Phillips crawled up to the ramp, tattered and bedraggled like refugees from chemical warfare.

"What's that?" Jeffries asked, nervously eyeing something hanging above the ramp. "Another booby trap?" It looked like a small hot air balloon made out of sheets crudely taped and sewn together.

"Maybe," Jared grumbled. "Jeffries, jam something into that pulley over there."

Jeffries jammed a stick tightly into the pulley.

Jared held up his crowbar. "All right, let's destroy this place!"

"*Aaaiiiaahhh!*" they yelled as they leaped across the ramp and began tearing apart everything in sight.

Inside the tree ship, Bruzelski pushed frantically against a lever. Something was wrong with the ship's electro-trashmatic, goonjammer defense array. Unnerved by all the crashing and bashing outside the door, she rushed into the nose of the ship and adjusted the view screen. There they were — the hideous gang of monsters — making pulp out of the entry landing. What was worse, the Star-Fighters' last line of defense — the balloon — was just hanging there doing nothing while the invaders walked around the trip wire as easy as you please.

A crash at the door sent Bruzelski reeling to the floor. "Open up, meatheads!" Jared's voice shouted. The hull buckled beneath Jared's blows.

Bruzelski was trapped. "MacIntyre!" she screamed. Shields were down, ship's defenses were inoperative, and the enemy was boarding.

At that moment, Beamer and Ghoulie pushed through the branches right above the tree ship's nose.

"Hey, look what we got perched in our tree," Ghoulie said, laughing. He pointed his camera at the four ooze-drenched boys. "Show time!"

"Somethin's wrong," Beamer said anxiously. It was clear that, however silly they looked, Jared's demolition squad was making toothpicks out of the door. "Why hasn't she dropped the goonjammer array?"

"That's why!" Ghoulie said, taking his eye from the camera's viewfinder. "The pulley's jammed!"

Beamer's eyes alighted on his mom's electrical conduit. His overly careful mom had anchored it in enough places to hold an aircraft carrier. Maybe it was the strangely haunting buzzing and chirping sounds that seemed to be getting louder, or maybe he'd watched too many GI Joe cartoons, or maybe he'd just had too much spinach for supper last night. But something had definitely triggered his usually suppressed hero mechanism, for Beamer suddenly wrestled off his T-shirt, draped it around the conduit and, holding tightly to each end, jumped. The next thing he knew, he was sliding down the conduit straight toward the balloon ... and Jared.

21

The Finger of God

Jared saw Beamer just as he slid by the balloon and kicked the stick off the pulley. Then Beamer slammed into the side of the ship and fell to the floor right in the middle of Jared's gang. Jared yanked Beamer up and slammed him against the tree ship door. The door, though, was already too far gone. It gave way, dumping Beamer to the floor inside with Jared smack on top of him.

"Beamer!" Scilla, no longer Lieutenant Bruzelski, yelled in surprise.

Jared's twisted features were close up in Beamer's face. "Where are those drawings?" he snarled.

"I don't have them," Beamer stammered, his life passing before his eyes like a second-rate cartoon.

"You took them. I know you did!" Jared ranted as he snatched Beamer up from the floor. "And I want them back or this tree house is splinters!"

"I told you, I don't have them! Not anymore," Beamer protested. Of course, Jared was about as likely to believe that Beamer had simply thrown them away as he was to launch a babysitting service.

"What does it matter?" Beamer stammered, trying a new tack. "They're good ... better than any eighth grader's I've ever seen. You could—"

"Yeah ... right. I've been down that road," Jared growled. "As soon as anybody sees you're different, you're gone, man. You're an outsider ... an alien."

He threw Beamer to the floor and picked up his crowbar.

He swung it about wildly. Plywood instrument panels cracked into smithereens; wires snapped apart, sparking.

"Jared!" Beamer and Scilla cried together, both lunging for him. But Jared merely flung Scilla down and stepped aside, allowing Beamer to plunge past him and across a table.

The windy noise outside had become much louder. Suddenly Jared's laughter choked off. A thick cloud of insects swarmed in the door. They seemed to ignore Beamer and Scilla—but not Jared.

"Get away!" he yowled, swatting at them. He spun around, slashing about wildly, and tripped out the door.

Outside, Jared found himself in a hurricane of insects—flying, jumping crickets, grasshoppers, katydids—hundreds of them—swarming around the yelping, swatting gang. They were pouring out of the balloon as if it was a cosmic black hole—a leaping, chirping, buzzing, furious barrage. And from every side, more came to join them. The tree was becoming one huge insect world.

Ghoulie, meanwhile, was gleefully recording every delicious detail of Jared's distress, zooming in for spicy close-ups, pulling back for wide-angle panoramas of this classic Kid vs. Bug Battle.

The balloon, having dropped its leaf and bug avalanche, billowed out. Now real balloons—the helium filled ones that had actually been holding up the sheet balloon—started spilling out from beneath the edge of the sheet. They flew up toward the cloudy sky, popping and exploding with all the noise of a fireworks display as they struck sharp twigs and pieces of bark.

Last of all, the sheet, finally emptied of its balloons, floated down to land on top of the boys—bugs and all—pushing their panic level up still another notch. But their efforts to escape only got them wound up together in a squirming, sticky, seed-covered cluster. Then they fell—in one rolling, yelping mass—taking the express route into the safety net far below.

Still whimpering and pawing at insects, real and imagined, they wrestled their way out of the sheet, crawled to the edge of the net, and dropped to the ground.

"Come on!" Beamer shouted to Ghoulie as he and Scilla dropped out from beneath the tree ship in their rope-swinging transporter/elevator.

"How's the action, Spielberg?" Beamer asked Ghoulie.

"I think we've got a hit," he answered, patting his camcorder proudly.

By the time they got to the street, Jared and his terrified flunkies were already halfway down the block. Ghoulie kept the camera rolling, taking one last long shot of the tattered remains of the Skullcross Gang.

By the time Ghoulie lowered his camera, Scilla had caught up with them. "We did it, y'all!" she shouted, breathing hard. "We did it!"

"You did most of it," Beamer said, giving her an extra high-five.

"You're not kidding," she threw back at him. "Hey! What took y'all so long, anyway?"

"A little miscalculation," Ghoulie said, rolling his eyes. "What I want to know, though, is where you got all those bugs? That was awesome!"

"Bugs? What are you talkin' about?" Scilla asked puzzled. "We didn't put in any bugs ... did we?"

"I don't know," Beamer shrugged. "Maybe the molasses attracted them or something."

"Gimme a break!" Ghoulie protested, "There must have

been thousands of bugs."

"I told you," Beamer said thoughtfully. "It's no ordinary tree." He turned and looked back down Murphy Street. "And this is no ordinary street."

The clouds parted to give the sun a last peek at the world before it dipped below the rooftops. A breeze ruffled through the leaves, making tap-dancing sounds as they brushed against each other. Beamer glanced at Parker's Castle. Already the lights were glowing in the deepening twilight. Standing in the third-story tower window was the same shadowy figure he had grown accustomed to seeing there.

"Jared won't be able to touch a Star-Fighter!" Ghoulie cheered. "Not after today." He tapped his camera as he snapped it carefully into its case.

Beamer settled into the "V" between two branches and took out his meteor fragment.

Ghoulie plopped down beside him. "I think you're right. That meteor did do something radical to this tree. It made it into a self-contained world with its own ecosystem! And, what's more, that energy field seems to reject certain brain-wave patterns—the ones that come from people that Ms. Parker said had 'malice' in their hearts."

"So you're saying that the tree thinks Jared is a germ and spits him out?"

"Sort of, but this is the really cool part: I think that people with matching brainwave patterns add to the energy in the field. That's how we get those way-out adventures."

"The finger of God," Beamer mumbled as he juggled the stone in his hand. "Yep, I don't know how or why, but God touched us through this little rock from another world."

"One of those 'mysterious ways,' huh," Scilla chimed

in.

"Yeah, I got a feelin' God's got all kinds of mysterious

Scilla

Beamer

Ghoulie

called out, "Beam me up!" As he moved upward through the branches, he heard once again the buzzing of the insects. But something was different. *The crickets*, it suddenly occurred to him. *They're singing. The crickets are finally singing.*

Character Bios

Priscilla Bruzelski:
Age: 12 / 6th grade, Hair/Eyes: dishwater-blonde/green, Height: 4'9"

"*Scilla*" refuses to be called by her full name because it's too prissy for this tomboy. She is smaller than your average twelve-year-old, but she makes up for her small stature with a fiercely independent, feisty personality. She lives with her grandmother whom she was sent to live with when her single mother remarried. She has a half-brother named Dashiell who lives with her mother and her mother's new husband. Her grandmother takes her to church every Sunday out of tradition. Scilla loves climbing trees, football, basketball, and anything that's not girly. She doesn't get along with the popular girls at school, but she doesn't mind. She has strong opinions and will fight for what she believes is right.

Benson McIntyre:
Age: 13 / 7th grade, Hair/Eyes: short, wavy, sandy brown hair/blue, Height: 5'

"*Beamer*," named from the famous "Beam me up Scotty" line in *Star Trek*, has an interest in all things science fiction. He hates his given name, so don't call him Benson. You might get a response in wry, sarcastic humor from this energetic teenager. He recently moved with his family from Southern California to Middle America. He has a younger brother named Michael and an older sister named Erin. His father, referred to as "Mr. Mac," is a theater director, and his mother is a pediatrician called "Dr. Mac." He loves playing on the computer, likes keeping up with the times, and considers himself on the cutting edge. Coming from a strong Christian family, he analyzes all problems with deep spiritual thought. His love for science extends to his speech, as he often speaks in sci-fi space metaphors.

Garfunkel Ives:
Age: 12 / 7th grade, Hair/Eyes: black/brown, Height: 4'10"

"*Ghoulie*" got his name from the wide-eyed look he makes when he is excited. He's an intelligent boy who skipped a grade. He's small for his age and is the typical nerd who loves gadgets and computers, which makes him fodder for bullies. The constant bullying makes him jaded and sarcastic, and he would love to get revenge on the bullies. His father is a successful CFO of a large corporation and his mother is a highly-respected lawyer. His parents have little time for a spiritual life — or him — and have left his upbringing to the nanny. His parents have also left him with an extensive computer and gadget collection which he loves to use to quench his thirst for scientific knowledge.

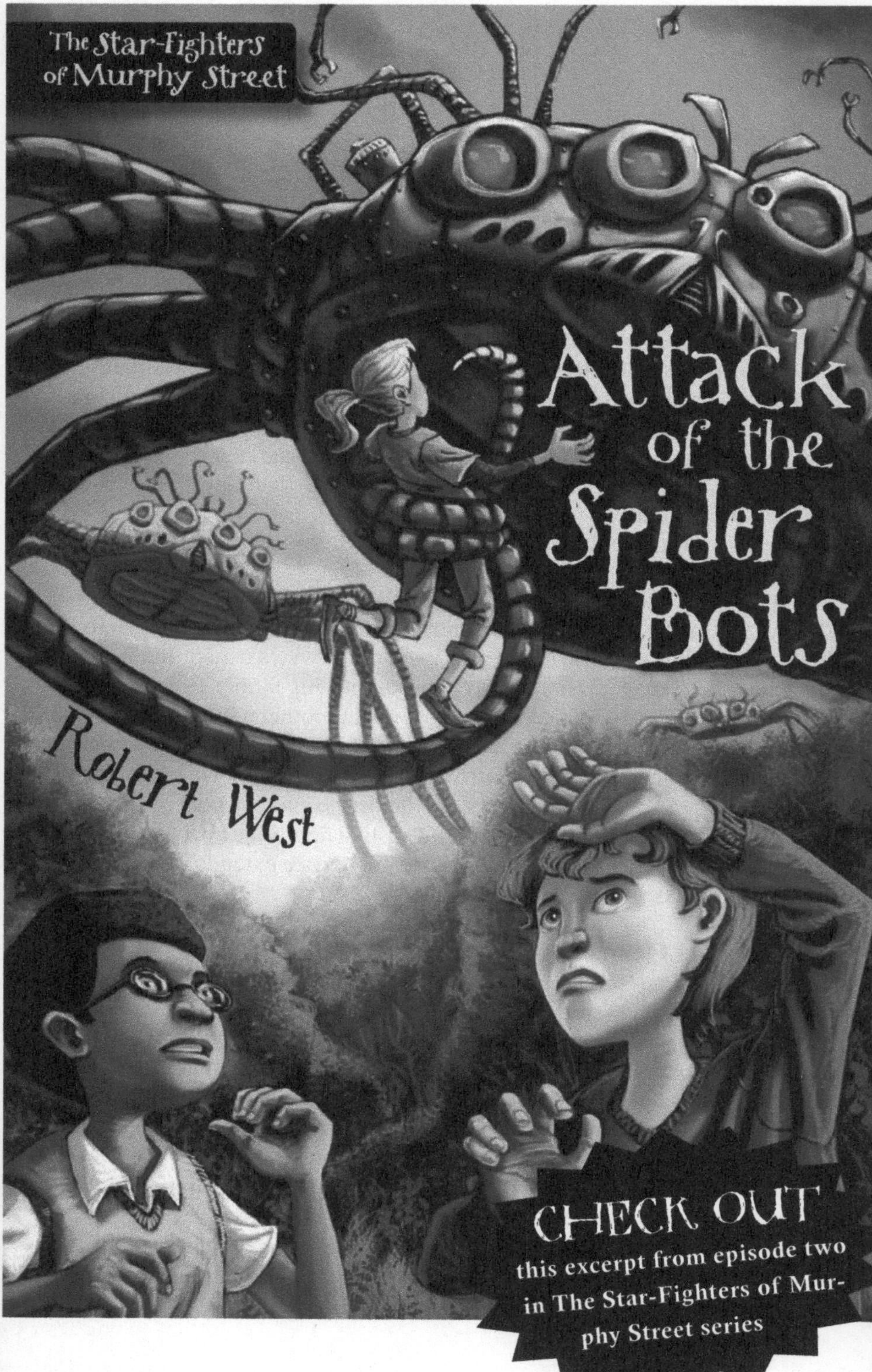
The Star-Fighters
of Murphy Street
Attack
of the
Spider
Bots
Robert West
CHECK OUT
this excerpt from episode two
in The Star-Fighters of Mur-
phy Street series

1

The Cave of the Beast

Becoming a teenager is like living in a sci-fi movie. You keep morphing into somebody else while emergencies are popping up all around you.

Case in point: Beamer tripped on the rock steps leading into their secret cave network. As Ghoulie figured out later, it was because Beamer's leg had morphed one-eighth inch longer than it had been the last time he climbed those steps. Then while Beamer was rubbing his scraped knee, Scilla picked up a faint noise. They listened until they heard a distant rumble and a repeating clank.

They called themselves Star-Fighters—Beamer, the exile from California; Ghoulie, the African-American brain trust;

and Scilla, the girl who could do anything a boy could, only better. They got the name because of the spaceship they found high up in Beamer's tree. It didn't seem like much at first. After all, it was only a ramshackle wooden tree house shaped like a spaceship—no graphics card, no 3-D accelerator, nothing you could shove into an Xbox. But, hey! You know what they say about looks being deceiving. That broken-down plywood box had already taken them to places no kid has gone before. And, in the process, they were finding a lot of strange worlds right where they lived—that being an ancient, pothole-ridden lane, only one block long, named Murphy Street. This cave labyrinth was one of those weird worlds.

Up till now, though, they'd used the caves mostly as just a shortcut home from school. But an unexplained clank, Beamer thought, was a good reason to start some big-time exploring. After all, a rumble could be lots of things—an earthquake, rushing water, whatever. A clank, though, was something else. Nothing in nature clanked.

So they were off. Beamer and Ghoulie were following Scilla, who was holding a lamp to light the way. She tracked the clanking and rumbling sounds up, around, and through the winding, cobweb-infested network of caves beneath Murphy Street. Luckily there weren't that many bugs, rats, and mice in winter. As usual, Scilla led them to a dead end.

"Scillaaaaa!" Beamer complained, remembering the time Scilla had led them into a brick wall when they were being chased by Jared and his bully goons. Now they were facing an unmovable rock wall. Actually, it was a pretty interesting wall. Symbols and pictures had been scratched or painted all over it—Native American, he guessed.

"Hey, it's not my fault!" Scilla protested. Putting her ear to the wall, she listened and then continued, "Don't you hear it? The clanking sounds are coming from the other side of the wall!"

After putting their ears to the wall, Beamer and Ghoulie had to agree that Scilla was right. "Okay, Plan B," Ghoulie said. "The Indiana Jones maneuver." As if the wall was one big pinball machine, they started punching and pulling every symbol and protruding rock they saw, looking for a trigger that would open a hidden door.

Finally, when their fingers were seriously throbbing, they stopped. "There's got to be another way in there," Beamer said, blowing on his finger. "Let's backtrack."

That's what they did until the found a side tunnel. Careful to scratch little rocket symbols into the wall so that they could find their way back, they again struck off into the unknown. Making one turn after another, trying to head in the direction of the clanking sound, they fought through major spider colonies and piles of rubble. Suddenly they heard another sound, this one loud and shrill. Scilla stopped abruptly and shouted, "Go back!" But it was too late. The next thing they knew there was a one-eyed creature with bad breath wailing like a banshee hot on their behinds. That's *hot* as in "burn-your-buns hot" and getting hotter by the second. The Star-Fighters ran down a dark tunnel as fast as their middle-school legs could go, which wasn't all that fast since they had to run bending over like orangutans. The trouble was that the tunnel was so small they couldn't stand up—not even Scilla. Frankly their prospects didn't look good. In fact, you might want to see if anything is written on the rest of the pages. This could turn out to be a very short story.

Just an hour before, on their way home from school, the threesome had decided to take their subterranean shortcut. It wasn't all that short when you considered that they had to take a long ladder beneath the park, wind through a maze of caves, and then come back up and cut through a bizarre garden behind Parker's Castle. That "Castle" was Murphy Street's own little corner of Transylvania—dark towers, moat, and all. It belonged to Ms. Parker, who just happened to be the scariest person on the street.

Shortcut or not, that passage beneath Murphy Street had saved their hides more than once. It was their emergency escape route and their hideaway from bullying gangs. This summer, the caves had been lit up like Christmas from the clouds of fireflies and the moss glowing on the walls. With the coming of winter, though, the fireflies were burrowing into their tiny winter caves, leaving only the dim, creepy glow of the moss for illumination. That might be enough if you're a bat, but not if you're human.

Luckily the lanterns still worked, if you could really call them lanterns. After all, lanterns were supposed to have a flame, right? These didn't; instead, when you turned one on, it had a large round bulb filled with glowing liquid. The eerie part, though, was that the light was the same color as a firefly's light. Of course, the really eerie part was that no one knew who made them or how they worked. But somebody had made enough of them to place all over the caves so that you could find one when you needed it.

That was a good thing, since you couldn't always count on

having a flashlight when an emergency turned up—like the one they were having now.

The bad news was that a lantern had guided them into the tunnel they were now wishing they could find a way out of. The good news? . . . They were still young, and their parents could probably get discounts on their tombstones.

The beast was almost on them, with its hot, steamy breath making them feel like shrimp on a barbie. Suddenly the tunnel floor slipped out from beneath them.

"Aiiiiiiiiii!" they cried as they flailed momentarily in midair. Then they fell. The next thing they knew, they were plunging through a chute—as in a water ride—and splashing into a fast-moving stream. The sound echoed all around them. They had the sense of being in a large space.

"Help, help!" Ghoulie burbled as he splashed the water frantically. "I can't swim!" Then he saw Scilla standing up, hands on hips, looking down at him with a smirk. He felt his knees bump against the streambed and stood, giving Scilla a sheepish, red-faced look.

"What was that thing?" Beamer sputtered as he crawled, drenched and muttering, out of the stream.

"I don't know," said Scilla, "but it could use some work on personal hygiene. I can still smell its breath."

"Next question," Ghoulie said as he peered through the darkness. "Where are we?"

A faint light grew in the distance . . . behind a range of hills.

"Are we outside?" asked Scilla. "It can't be night already."

"Worse than that. It looks like sunrise," groaned Beamer.

"It's almost time for school."

A soft line of light slowly crawled across the landscape, revealing more hills and valleys, then roads and a village. There was a church with a steeple, a train station, shops—some with windmills—and a group of houses.

"One thing's for sure," said Scilla. "We're not in Middleton anymore."

Something didn't seem right about the scenery. Beamer couldn't quite put his finger on it. Again they heard the beast scream, and they whirled around to see the one-eyed monster charge across a double-arched bridge.

"It's . . . it's a train!" cried Ghoulie.

Now there was enough light to see that the eye was the headlamp for a steam locomotive. *Looks about the size of our living room sofa*, thought Beamer. That was when he realized what was wrong—the scenery was miniaturized!

"Holy tamole! D'y'all mean we're trapped in somebody's train set?" asked Scilla.

Attack of the Spider-Bots: Episode II
Softcover • ISBN 978-0-310-71426-2

Star-Fighters Beamer, Ghoulie, and Scilla follow a strange clanking sound in their cave labyrinth and stumble onto a screaming one-eyed monster that chases them into a huge cavern enclosing a fully animated miniature world. Their search for the person who created that world leads them on a wild adventure to a palatial mansion within a wintry jungle that hides a terrible secret—a secret that they will have to trust God to expose.

Available now at your local bookstore!

Escape from the Drooling Octopod!: Episode III
Softcover • ISBN 978-0-310-71427-9

The Star-Fighters, under attack from pink goblins and Molgotha, a drooling giant octo-pod, must save a girl locked in a "pink palace." In a wacky adventure which takes them to a pink planet, through subterranean civilizations and into a modern day Dr. Franken-stein's laboratory, the Star-Fighters learn of the temptation to play God when faith is challenged and discover beauty in the most unlikely beasts.

Available now at your local bookstore!